Lord Deverill's Secret

Books by Amanda Grange

MR. KNIGHTLEY'S DIARY
LORD DEVERILL'S SECRET
HARSTAIRS HOUSE

Lord Deverill's Secret

Amanda Grange

BERKLEY SENSATION, NEW YORK

THE BERKLEY PUBLISHING GROUP
Published by the Penguin Group
Penguin Group (USA) Inc.
375 Hudson Street, New York, New York 10014, USA
Penguin Group (Canada), 90 Eglinton Avenue East, Suite 700, Toronto, Ontario M4P 2Y3, Canada
(a division of Pearson Penguin Canada Inc.)
Penguin Books Ltd., 80 Strand, London WC2R 0RL, England
Penguin Group Ireland, 25 St. Stephen's Green, Dublin 2, Ireland (a division of Penguin Books Ltd.)
Penguin Group (Australia), 250 Camberwell Road, Camberwell, Victoria 3124, Australia
(a division of Pearson Australia Group Pty. Ltd.)
Penguin Books India Pvt. Ltd., 11 Community Centre, Panchsheel Park, New Delhi—110 017, India
Penguin Group (NZ), 67 Apollo Drive, Rosedale, North Shore 0632, New Zealand
(a division of Pearson New Zealand Ltd.)
Penguin Books (South Africa) (Pty.) Ltd., 24 Sturdee Avenue, Rosebank, Johannesburg 2196,
South Africa

Penguin Books Ltd., Registered Offices: 80 Strand, London WC2R 0RL, England

LORD DEVERILL'S SECRET

Copyright © 2005 by Amanda Grange
Cover art by Aleta Rafton
Cover design by George Long
Text design by Tiffany Estreicher

First American edition: November 2007
Originally published in Great Britain by Robert Hale Ltd. in 2005.

Berkley Sensation trade paperback ISBN: 978-0-425-21772-6

PRINTED IN THE UNITED STATES OF AMERICA

10 9 8 7 6 5 4 3 2 1

For Gerda

CHAPTER ONE

Miss Cassandra Paxton put on her spencer and settled her bonnet on her golden head, then turned to her maid.

"Lord Deverill lives on the Steyne. It's time for us to pay him a visit."

"I don't like it," grumbled Moll. "You was brought up proper, Miss Cassie. You shouldn't be going visiting gennulmen on your own."

"I'm not on my own," teased Cassandra as she picked up her parasol. "I'm with you."

She opened the door and the two of them stepped out into the summer morning. Standing on the top step, she breathed in deeply, inhaling the tang of salt that was carried to her on the breeze, and lifted her face skyward as the cry of gulls filled the air.

"I'd forgotten how much I loved being in Brighton," she said. "I shouldn't have stayed away for so long."

"That's a fact. The house is in a muddle, being as how it was left shut up for a year," said Moll, adding dourly, "It's a wonder we haven't got rats."

"Well, we haven't," said Cassandra, who was used to Moll's grumblings and ignored her gloomy manner. "But you're right about the muddle. We will have to clean the house and tidy it from top to bottom when we return."

"A rare treat," said Moll, in an aggrieved tone of voice.

Cassandra led Moll down the narrow street then turned a corner. In front of them lay the sea. It was spread out like a piece of watered silk, undulating gently towards the horizon in a blaze of brilliant blue that reflected the clear blue sky. Fishing boats were dotted here and there on its surface, and their colourful sails blew in the breeze. Nearer to hand, more boats were drawn up on the shore, and next to them fishermen were mending their nets. A nursemaid was walking past them, keeping a watchful eye on a little boy who was playing with the waves.

"When we reach Lord Deverill's house, I want you to be quiet and let me speak," said Cassandra, as she and Moll began to walk along the sea front.

"Yes, miss, I'll keep my mouth shut," Moll grumbled, "but don't say as I didn't warn you if Lord Deverill tries to take advantage of you."

"As if you'd let him," returned Cassandra.

Moll had been her nurse for many years and had stayed on with the family, becoming first of all a housekeeper and then a maid of all work. She had comforted Cassandra when her parents had died and again when her brother had died, and Cassandra knew that Moll was utterly devoted.

"I think I'll go bathing tomorrow," said Cassandra, as they walked past a row of bathing huts pulled up on the beach.

"Nasty habit," said Moll with a shudder. "Climbing up them steps. Riding in a hut. Bumping over that beach on those big wheels and all to get into the water. If you wants a bath you can have one at home like a respectable body, instead of frolicking about in your chemise."

Cassandra twirled her parasol. "But it's not so easy to swim in the bath," she teased.

"If you drowns yourself, don't come complaining to me," said Moll, determined to have the last word.

It was not long before they reached the Steyne, a large grassy area set at right angles to the beach. It was empty apart from a footman who was hurrying across it, and who stopped to exchange a word with a lusty milkmaid before hurrying on. Its emptiness reminded Cassandra of how early it was and she felt a moment of doubt. It might be impossible for her to see Lord Deverill because he might not yet have risen. Living in the country, she had forgotten that the fashionable people in Brighton kept different hours, but she had gone too far to turn back. Summoning her courage she went up to the door of Lord Deverill's house. She lifted the lion's head knocker. It seemed to grin as she dropped it with a loud clang. She fiddled with her reticule as she waited patiently for the door to open, but nothing happened.

"Just as well," said Moll with dour relish. "Now we can go home again."

But just as she turned away from the door, it opened, and a superior butler stood there. He lifted one eyebrow when he saw Cassandra, then his gaze passed on to Moll.

"Yes?" he enquired.

"I am here to see Lord Deverill," said Cassandra.

He lifted his eyebrow even further.

"Lord Deverill is not at home," he said in a stately fashion.

"Then I will wait until he returns," said Cassandra firmly.

The butler looked as though he was about to say that Lord Deverill was not in need of another barque of frailty when he caught Moll's eye and changed his mind. He stood aside.

"If you will wait here," he said, as he allowed Cassandra into the hall. "I will see if his lordship has returned."

Cassandra looked around her as the butler disappeared. Like all town houses, it was comparatively small, but there was no denying that it was elegant. A number of prints lined the walls, and a vase of flowers was arranged attractively on a console table. Three x-frame stools were pushed back against the wall, and beyond them a modest staircase led upwards. The baluster was made of mahogany and the treads had been polished until they shone. She had time to notice nothing more before the butler returned and said, "Lord Deverill will give you five minutes of his time."

Cassandra followed him up the stairs and into the drawing-room. It was an elegant apartment, decorated in shades of gold and green, and was surprisingly spacious. There was an impressive marble fireplace, over which was hung a painting of the sea. The windows were large and damask curtains arranged themselves in sumptuous folds as they fell to the floor. To the side of the fireplace was a wing chair and there, sitting in his shirt and breeches, with a large hound at his feet, was Lord Deverill.

Her eyebrows lifted in surprise and she halted, momentarily taken aback. He was not at all what she had expected. She had thought he would be much younger, about twenty-two or three years of age, with dissolute features and a wild air, instead of which he was about thirty years of age. His hair was dark and his eyes were a clear sage green. His features were craggy, with a broad forehead and a strong nose and chin, but something about his mouth suggested that he could be good humoured if he pleased. He looked up as he saw her, and for a fleeting moment she thought she saw a glint of recognition in his eye. But that was absurd. He had never met her.

He stood up and said to his butler, "Thank you, Manby. That will be all."

"Very good, my lord."

"Won't you sit down?" he asked Cassandra, when the door closed behind the butler.

"Thank you."

Cassandra settled herself on the sofa and Moll sat down on a Chippendale chair by the door. Lord Deverill resumed his seat, crossing his feet at the ankle. He looked at her thoughtfully.

"Now, how may I help you, Miss . . . ?"

"Paxton," said Cassandra. "I've come to speak to you about my brother, my lord." Did she imagine it, or did something wary come into his eyes? She pressed on. "I found a letter when I was going through his things—" He looked surprised. "I know it's a year since he died, but I didn't have the heart to turn out his pockets at the time," she explained. "I've come to ask you if you know what it means."

She took the letter out of her reticule and handed it to him.

"As you can see, in it Rupert says he has done something terrible. I have been haunted by visions of a"—she hesitated, and then went on—"a young lady seduced and left without support."

"Miss Cassie!" exploded Moll, rising to her feet.

"Sit down, Moll," she said impatiently. "This is no time to be missish." She turned to Lord Deverill. "You knew

Rupert. Do you know what happened? Is there some young lady in desperate circumstances because of my brother's actions? If there is, I mean to do what I can to help her, and if she has no one else to turn to, she is welcome to come and live with me."

He looked at her for a long moment, his face unreadable, then he handed the letter back to her.

"I shouldn't worry. It was probably nothing. He doesn't speak of harming anyone. He probably meant that he had drunk too much, or lost more than he wanted to, gambling."

Cassandra felt a flood of relief.

"If that's all he meant . . . but do you know for sure?"

He regarded her as though deciding what to say, then said, "You may rest assured that no young ladies have been left destitute by your brother."

"Thank you." She smiled. "You have set my mind at rest. I mean to ask his other friends," she said, rising, "but if they tell me the same then I will be able to forget the matter."

"I shouldn't go and see them if I were you," said Lord Deverill, rising, too.

"Oh? Why not?"

"Because they are not all of them . . . reputable."

"I am not fresh from the schoolroom—"

"No?" he asked, lifting one eyebrow.

"No. I am two and twenty, and I am not ignorant of the ways of the world. I know my brother was a little wild, and I know that his friends are likely to be a little wild as well. I don't mean to bother them, merely to ask them if they know what my brother meant. Perhaps you can tell me where I can find them? Mr. Peter Raistrick, and Mr. Geoffrey Goddard?"

He thought for a minute and then said, "Goddard's out of town at the moment, but Mr. Raistrick is to be found in all the usual places. You will see him if you attend any of the assemblies."

"Thank you. I am going to the Castle Inn this evening. I will hope to see him there. And now I must take up no more of your time."

The butler entered.

"Mr. Standish, my lord."

"No need to announce me, Manby, I—"

The fair young man who had entered stopped short as he saw Cassandra.

"Pray don't heed me," she said. "My maid and I are just leaving."

And with this she left the room, leaving Lord Deverill and Mr. Standish looking after her.

"Tell me I'm dreaming," said Matthew Standish, as the door closed behind Cassandra.

"No. You're not." Justin, Lord Deverill drew his attention away from the door and gave it to his friend.

"What was she doing here?"

Justin leant against the marble mantelpiece.

"She came to ask me about Rupert."

Matthew stiffened.

"She found a letter in one of Rupert's pockets when she was going through his things. In it, he said he'd done something terrible," Justin said.

Matthew flinched. "Did he say what?"

"No, thank God. The letter was unfinished, and he never posted it. He wrote it in a drunken stupor, I would guess, and then stuffed it into his breeches pocket, forgetting all about it the next morning."

"And soon afterwards, he was dead. What did Cassandra want?"

"She wanted to know whether he'd seduced a young lady and left her destitute. She wanted to help the young lady if that was the case."

"Help her?" Matthew looked surprised. "That doesn't sound like a Paxton, wanting to help someone else."

"She might not be like her brother," said Justin, his eyes returning to the door.

"And she might be exactly the same. What did you tell her?"

"That she had no need to worry. That Rupert didn't leave any desperate women behind."

Matthew breathed a sigh of relief. "Disaster avoided."

"Not quite."

Matthew looked at him questioningly.

"She's going to see the rest of Rupert's friends. She wants to ask them if they know what he was talking about before she is satisfied."

"Hm. That could prove difficult. And just which of Rupert's friends does she know about?"

"I'm not sure. She mentioned Peter Raistrick and Geoffrey Goddard."

"She should be safe enough with them."

"She should. As long as it goes no further."

"So what are you going to do about it?" asked Matthew, sauntering over to a sofa and throwing himself down in a negligent attitude.

"I'm going to have her watched. See where she goes and who she speaks to."

"That's a good idea." Matthew looked up at Justin. "Because if she stirs up the past, she could put us in danger."

"Yes, she could," agreed Justin thoughtfully. "Mortal danger. And not just us, but herself. I can't let that happen. If things go too far—"

"Yes?" asked Matthew.

Justin's face became set. "Then I will have to deal with it."

~ ~ ~

Cassandra felt light of heart as she and Moll walked back to the town house. Her interview with Lord Deverill had gone well. He had agreed to see her, treated her with courtesy, and set her mind at ease. But there had been something. . . . She frowned. She did not know what it was, but there had been something wary about him; something cautious, or even hostile, that had not seemed quite right.

"A fine gennulmen," said Moll approvingly, breaking into her thoughts.

"Yes, indeed," said Cassandra slowly.

"A fine friend for Master Rupert," said Moll, shaking her head to express her sorrow over the abrupt curtailment of the friendship.

"Yes."

Cassandra was thoughtful. She could not see why the two of them had been friends. She could not see that they had had anything in common, for anyone less like Rupert would have been difficult to imagine: Rupert with his wild ways, his love of pleasure, and his indulgence in excess; Lord Deverill, with his restraint . . . He had not been completely honest with her, she was sure of it. His answers to her questions had been guarded. But perhaps it was simply that he had been afraid she would ask awkward questions about her brother's drinking habits or mistresses, questions he would rather avoid.

Dismissing the subject, she turned her attention back to her surroundings. The Steyne was busier now. A number of gentlemen were exercising their horses, and several ladies were heading towards the circulating library, followed by footmen with arms full of books. Ignoring Moll's advice that she should accept Lord Deverill's assurance and not trouble any more of Rupert's friends, and likewise ignoring Moll's dire warnings that her mother would turn in her grave if she asked any more questions about "women what was no better than they ought to be," Cassandra walked down to the sea front. She felt her spirits lift as she enjoyed the beauty of her surroundings. She loved Brighton. The air was always fresh, and the fashionable people walking to and fro gave it an air of prosperity. She turned right and strolled along by the water, at last returning to her town house. As she approached it, she saw that a carriage was drawn up in front of it, and sitting inside it was one of her oldest friends, Maria.

"There you are," Maria greeted her, stepping out of the carriage as Cassandra drew level with it. "I have knocked on the door three times already and I was about to go home. I thought I must have misremembered the date of your arrival."

Cassandra gave an inward sigh as she looked at Maria's wonderful outfit. As always, Maria was dressed in the latest fashions, and wore a darling peach spencer fastened over her muslin gown. A fetching bonnet, lined with ruched silk and decorated with a peach ribbon, was perched on her dark head. She was holding a new parasol in her hands, and her gloves were dyed to match her spencer.

I wish I could have something new, Cassandra thought, as she glanced down at her tight spencer and patched gloves.

Pushing the useless thought aside, she said, "No, I was out."

"So I see. Taking the air?" asked Maria.

"Visiting gennulmen," said Moll darkly.

"Gentlemen?" asked Maria, turning to Cassandra in surprise.

Cassandra's mouth quirked. "You had better come in."

Cassandra unlocked the door and led the way inside. She wished she had a butler to open the door and a row of footmen to greet her guests, but such luxuries were beyond her. John the coachman was the one male servant she could afford, and even he was absent at present as he was busy with the coach-maker. So she took on the role of a servant herself, not for the first time, waiting until they were all in the hall then closing the door behind them.

Moll started to follow Cassandra into the parlour.

"Thank you, Moll," she said firmly.

"Meaning as how I'm to get on with the dusting, I suppose," grumbled Moll.

"Meaning you're not to tell Maria anything I don't want her to know," said Cassandra with a dimple.

Moll retreated, still grumbling, to the kitchen.

"What gentlemen have you been visiting?" asked Maria, agog, as she followed Cassandra into the parlour.

"Only one." Cassandra took off her battered bonnet and patted her hair, then set her bonnet down on a chair. "Lord Deverill."

"Lord Deverill!"

"Yes. Why, do you know him?"

"I know of him. Who doesn't? He's one of the most eligible bachelors in Brighton. He might be poor, but an earl is an earl. Miss Kerrith has set her cap at him, and so has Miss Langley, and half a dozen others besides. You should see them every time he walks into a room, simpering and flirting and fluttering their fans! And their mothers are not much better! They know he needs to marry an heiress, and they are determined to catch him. But what were you doing visiting him? I hope you didn't go alone? You'll have no reputation left."

"Of course not," said Cassandra, removing her spencer. "I went with Moll."

"Moll!" Maria removed her bonnet and spencer likewise. "Moll isn't enough to protect your reputation. You should have taken Harry and me."

"Would you have gone?" asked Cassandra.

"Well, no," Maria admitted. "Harry would have refused."

"Which is why I didn't tell you. I'm sorry not to take you into the drawing-room," Cassandra continued, looking round the homely room with a touch of chagrin, "but it isn't habitable. This is the only room Moll and I have cleaned so far."

"It doesn't matter. It's you I came to see, not the house. You shouldn't have stayed away so long," said Maria, sitting down on a faded chaise longue. "Harry and I have been hoping you would visit all year. We have missed you. When your parents were alive you came to Brighton every year. Now we have to make do with you whenever we are lucky enough to have you. I hope you mean to stay?"

"For a little while, yes. Long enough to settle some . . . private business . . . and clean the town house," said Cassandra.

"And enjoy yourself, I hope," said Maria. "Now that your period of mourning is over, we hope to see much more of you."

"Unfortunately not."

The time had come to tell Maria that she meant to sell the house. She felt a pang as she glanced round the room, reliving her earliest memories. As her gaze wandered over the chair by the window, she could almost see her mother sitting and sewing there. She smiled as she remembered her mother pricking her finger and sucking it, saying that she was a poor needlewoman, and exhorting Cassandra and Lizzie to become better ones. Cassandra's gaze moved on towards the fireplace, as she remembered how her father had liked to sit by the fire, reading his newspaper and grumbling about the government. She glanced at the table, recalling the way Rupert had sat there, lolling indolently across it after a night's dissipation. And in her mind's eye she saw nine-year-old Lizzie dancing round the room, twirling around happily to show off a new frock.

She gave an inward sigh and banished the visions. Steeling herself to say what must be said, she continued, "Maria, I can't keep the town house. I have come here to clean it, and then to sell it."

Maria looked horrified. "Cassie! No!"

"I have to," said Cassandra. "It's mortgaged, and I can no longer afford to keep it. Besides, if I sell it, I can use the proceeds to pay off the mortgage on the estate."

She had been left the estate on her brother's death as luckily it had not been entailed. Her father had willed it to her brother, making the provision that if Rupert died before he had an heir, the estate was to pass to Cassandra. But it was heavily mortgaged, and difficult to maintain.

"You are not thinking clearly," said Maria, shaking her head. "You can't deprive yourself and Lizzie of a house by the sea. It is very good for your health, and Lizzie loves it so."

"I know, but I am thinking of Lizzie as much as myself. I don't want her to grow up in poverty. I want her to be able to have the things I had when I was a little girl. I want her to be able to keep her pony, and to have some new clothes from time to time. You cannot imagine how dreadful I felt last week when I packed her valise for her visit to her school friend. Her chemises were all cut down from mine, and every single gown she had was either scorched or mended."

"I understand," said Maria affectionately. "It isn't easy for you, I know. But why not marry? You're very beautiful and you will soon find a husband. There are any number of eligible gentlemen in Brighton. A husband will take care of all that sort of thing for you."

"I have thought about it, but decided against it. A husband is unlikely to welcome Lizzie. I don't want her to be banished to the schoolroom or treated like an interloper, or even worse, forced to remain at school for the holidays. I want her to have a happy home and a loving upbringing, as I had."

"Some men might welcome her, as your sister," said Maria optimistically.

"If I meet one, I promise to consider his offer if he makes me one," said Cassandra, "but until then, I must do what I can to provide for her, and for myself."

Maria nodded. "Then we must make sure we fit as much as we can into your visit. We'll patronize the best shops along North Street and promenade along the Steyne. We'll ride on the Downs and visit all the local beauty spots, and we'll visit some of the nearby grand houses—when the families are away, they allow their housekeepers to show people round, and Harry and I often go visiting. We'll go to Devil's Dyke and go swimming in the sea . . . and then you'll remember how much you love Brighton and be determined never to leave it!"

Cassandra smiled but shook her head.

"I won't tease you anymore," said Maria. "Tell me, how did you find Lord Deverill," she went on, changing the subject. "What was he like?"

Cassandra played with her short, puffed sleeve and considered.

"He was not what I expected him to be. He was about thirty years of age, with a forbidding countenance and an air of command. He is, I would guess, a man who likes to have his own way."

"Don't they all! They are born that way, I fear. Even Harry! It is one of the worst things about them. But why did you go to see him? It seems an odd thing to do."

"Because he was a friend of Rupert's." She frowned. "He was nothing like Rupert. I cannot think what they had in common."

"They were probably drinking partners, or gambling cronies," said Maria. "Men mean a great deal by the word friend, but none of it is what we would mean. If they can get drunk with a fellow and ride as hard as him, then they call him friend."

"You are probably right," said Cassandra.

"Even so," said Maria thoughtfully, "now that you have met him, he might continue the acquaintance. Of course, it isn't to be relied upon. He might cut you just as easily. But if you see him at the assemblies, he might ask you to dance. You are coming to the assembly rooms with us this evening?"

"Of course. I have my dress all ready."

"It's not the jonquil satin, I hope?" asked Maria, pulling a face. "That has never suited you, and it's far too small."

"No. Not the jonquil satin: the white muslin."

"Oh, yes, that will be very suitable, even if it is abominably old. I remember seeing you wear it years ago, but no one here has seen it, so it will not signify."

"Although I feel wrong dressing as a young girl, when I've been the mistress of an estate for a year," said Cassandra.

"You sound like an elderly matron!" said Maria with a laugh. "You are only two and twenty, Cassie. Hardly in your dotage! It will do you good to go to the assembly. You have had too much sadness and worry of late. It will give you a chance to be young."

"Yes, it will," said Cassandra with a sudden smile. "I am looking forward to it."

CHAPTER TWO

My dearest Lizzie.

It was later that day, in the early evening, and Cassandra was sitting in her bedroom at her Sheraton writing desk. She dipped her quill into the ink and then carried on with her letter.

Moll and I had an exciting start to our visit when the wheel came off our coach. Fortunately, John managed to mend it temporarily and we were soon on our way, but it meant we arrived here later than we had expected, and after finishing the food we'd brought with us in the hamper, we went to bed. This morning John took the coach to be repaired properly and . . .

She hesitated, and then, leaving out all mention of Lord Deverill, wrote:

. . . Maria called on me. I am going to the assembly rooms with her this evening. Harry is taking us, and he has promised to dance with me.

"Time to be getting dressed," said Moll, entering the bed chamber with a can of hot water.

Cassandra laid her quill aside and went into the dressing room, where Moll poured hot water into the porcelain bowl on the washstand. Twigs of lavender poured out with it, filling the air with a delicious scent. Cassandra removed her wrapper and then washed in the fragrant water before putting on her chemise and dressing in her muslin gown. It was her last good gown, and had been bought just over three years before, shortly before the death of her parents. The high waist was ornamented with satin ribbon, and a matching ribbon trimmed the short puffed sleeves. At the back, a train flowed along the floor.

Moll fastened it for her and then dressed her hair, twisting it into a becoming chignon, and arranged a row of soft curls around her face. Cassandra glanced at herself in the cheval glass to check that she was tidy, then fastened a simple string of pearls around her neck. She pulled on her long evening gloves, smoothing them over her arms.

"You look lovely, Miss Cassie. Your Mama'd be proud," said Moll gruffly.

Cassandra gave her an impulsive hug.

"Thank you, Moll."

The sound of a carriage pulling up outside the house drifted through the open window. Cassandra picked up her gauze shawl and her fan, then went downstairs and out to the waiting carriage.

"I am looking forward to this," said Maria, as Cassandra joined her in the carriage.

Beside her sat Harry. At twenty-eight years old, he was five years older than Maria. He had a good-natured countenance surrounded by glossy chestnut hair, and was dressed fashionably in a black tailcoat and cream knee breeches.

"Welcome back to Brighton," he said with a hearty smile. "Maria has been talking about nothing but your visit for the last two weeks. It's been, *When Cassie is here I'll do this,* and *When Cassie comes I'll do that* all the time."

"I'm very glad to be here," said Cassandra. "I've been looking forward to it as much as Maria has."

Cassandra took her place next to Maria, and they were on their way.

"Now don't forget, Captain Wade is the Master of Ceremonies," said Maria, as they reached the Castle Inn. "I don't believe you know him, but he's very influential in

Brighton, so you must hope he likes you. He runs the rooms with an iron hand, but he keeps us all in order."

"No, I don't know him," said Cassandra. "I've never been to the Castle before. I was too young when I used to come here with my parents, but they met there, and it was Captain Wade who introduced them."

"Then perhaps he might introduce you to your future husband!" said Maria airily.

Cassandra looked about her with interest as they arrived at the Castle and went inside. The chandeliers were already lit, and she could see that the rooms had a restrained elegance which formed a perfect backdrop to all the gaily dressed people. She was relieved to discover that her own outfit did not appear too much out of place, for although her dress was three years old, styles had changed very little in that space of time, and what had been suitable in 1802 looked equally well now in 1805. The older ladies wore coloured gowns, set off by the restraint of the gentlemen's black and blue coats, and here and there a flash of scarlet shone as an officer went in or out of the card-room.

"Mr. and Mrs. Winter, it is an honour to welcome you once again to the assembly rooms," said Captain Wade with a bow.

"We're delighted to be here," said Maria.

Captain Wade looked enquiringly at Cassandra.

"This is my friend, Miss Paxton," said Maria.

"Ah, yes, Mrs. Winter has told me so much about you. She has been looking forward to your visit for some time. I remember your parents well, and of course your brother, Miss Paxton. I hope you will have a pleasant evening with us."

"Thank you. I'm sure I shall," said Cassandra.

Captain Wade bowed and moved on to the next guests. Cassandra, Maria and Harry went further into the ballroom. At one end sat the musicians, and in the centre of the floor there was a set forming for a cotillion.

"Now, Harry, you must dance with Cassandra," said Maria, as they found a secluded spot at the side of the room.

"Nothing would give me greater pleasure," said Harry gallantly, offering Cassandra his arm.

As she took Harry's arm and went with him on to the dance floor, Cassandra looked about her. She was hoping to catch a glimpse of Peter Raistrick, or at least a young man who might be Peter, for she did not know him by appearance. She could see two or three young men who were suitable candidates.

"Do you know a Mr. Peter Raistrick?" she asked Harry, as she turned to face him and dropped him a curtsy.

Harry frowned. "Yes. I know him," he said.

"Is he here tonight?"

Harry glanced towards the side of the room, where a dissolute-looking young man was lounging.

"Is that him?" asked Cassandra.

"Yes," said Harry reluctantly.

"I'd like you to introduce me."

"He's not the right sort," said Harry. "You'd better leave him alone."

"He was a friend of Rupert's," Cassandra explained. "There is something I need to ask him. It won't take me long, and after that, I promise you I won't speak to him again."

"Oh, well, in that case," said Harry reluctantly.

Cassandra could tell that he didn't like it, but she was relieved that he had agreed to do as she asked. As soon as the dance was over, she would speak to Mr. Raistrick and find out if he could shed any light on her brother's letter.

~ ~ ~

At the far side of the ballroom, Justin saw Cassandra take to the floor with Harry. He had been at the assembly rooms for some time, having arrived unfashionably early, and he now watched her as she curtsied to Harry.

"She came, then."

Matthew Standish was standing next to him. He had arrived at the same time as Justin and now his eyes followed Cassandra's every move.

"Yes, she did, as I knew she would."

"You've warned Peter that she wants to talk to him, I take it?" asked Matthew.

"I have. He won't give us any trouble. He knows what to say."

Matthew turned to Justin.

"He knows what you want him to say, but can we trust him?"

"Yes. I'm sure of it. Peter isn't our problem. He can be relied upon." Justin's eyes moved across the floor, to where a middle-aged man with curly brown hair, simply dressed in tailcoat and knee breeches, was standing. "Our problem is Elwin."

Matthew followed his glance, then quickly looked away, fixing his eyes on a random pair of dancers.

"Do you think she knows about Elwin?" asked Matthew.

"No. I don't think so. She didn't mention him, in any case. But that doesn't mean that someone won't mention his name to her, and if that happens she might seek him out."

"It will be no good warning Elwin, I suppose?" asked Matthew dubiously.

"None at all. Elwin does as he pleases."

Matthew pursed his lips. "That could prove difficult for us."

Justin agreed. "Which is why it will be our job this evening to make sure they don't have a chance to meet each other. If Elwin makes a move towards her, or she towards him, then I'll step in and ask her to dance. If she's already danced with me, then it will be up to you."

"Very well," Matthew agreed. "Between us, we should manage to keep her occupied. What about supper?"

"I'll take her in. With her friend's husband on one side of her, and me on the other, we should be able to keep her away from any . . . less desirable . . . parties."

~ ~ ~

Cassandra dropped Harry a curtsy as the orchestra played the closing chords of the dance, then she took his arm as he led her across the floor to the far side of the room. She ran her eyes over Peter Raistrick. He was exactly the sort of young man she had pictured as one of Rupert's friends. He was extravagantly dressed in a blue coat, with a heavily embroidered waistcoat and satin knee breeches. His fair hair was brushed back from his face and he had amber eyes. He was attractive, but loose living was beginning to spoil his looks. His face was flushed and there was a suggestion of spread around the girth. His lips were loose and his eyes were hot.

"Raistrick, I'd like to introduce Miss Paxton," said Harry uncomfortably.

Peter pushed himself away from the pillar and stood up straight.

"Well, well, little Cassie," he said, then grinned. "You'll have to forgive me for calling you that. It was what Rupert always called you."

"I will leave you two to become better acquainted," said Harry, adding to Cassandra significantly, "I will not be far away if you need me."

"Well, well," said Peter again, when Harry had left. He spoke heartily, but there was an underlying wariness about him. "I didn't know you were in town. What are you doing in Brighton?"

"I'm visiting here for a few weeks," said Cassandra.

"That's a good idea. I always come here for the summer. When did you arrive?"

"Yesterday evening," said Cassandra.

"Are you planning to live here?" he asked casually.

"Alas, no. I'm afraid that at the end of the summer I will have to offer the town house for sale."

"Ah. It's a sad thing, economy," he said. "Rupert would have been saddened to know the house was going to be sold. He belonged here, in Brighton. He was very popular, you know. He was always eager for a game. We miss him badly."

"Thank you." Cassandra was glad he had had some good friends, even if they were dissolute. Her brother had spent the last year of his life in Brighton and had seldom returned to the estate, preferring to drink and gamble away the small income he had been left rather than trying to re-store his fortunes. It had caused her great concern and some anger, for whilst Rupert had had satin breeches and coats of superfine, Lizzie had been forced to wear cut-down clothes, but nevertheless she had loved her brother and was glad to know that he had had friends. "I never thought he would die like that," she said regretfully, thinking of his death.

"It's a bad thing, to die so young," said Peter sympathetically.

"To be thrown from his horse . . ." Cassandra shook her head. "He was always such a good horseman. He could ride almost before he could walk. He had an excellent seat, and I've seen him hang on when other men would have been thrown."

Peter shrugged. "It can happen to even the best of us. He took a hedge. There was a ditch beyond it. It was dark. He didn't see it."

Cassandra sighed.

"He had been drinking, I suppose."

Peter shrugged as if to say, *Young men like to drink.*

"I found a letter, when I was going through Rupert's things," said Cassandra, rousing herself from her thoughts.

"A letter?"

Peter looked up innocently.

"Yes. In it, Rupert said he had done something terrible," said Cassandra.

"He did?" Peter's voice was bland. "Do you have any idea of what he meant?"

"No."

"He didn't explain in the letter?" asked Peter.

"Unfortunately not. He never finished it. I found it folded up in his breeches pocket. I was hoping you could tell me what he meant."

"It was probably nothing. A bad bet," said Peter. "He liked to gamble on the races, but it's a tricky business, racing. It's easy to lose a fortune. I should know. I've lost a few fortunes myself."

He gave an uneasy laugh.

"Yes. Lord Deverill thought it must be something of the sort."

"You should listen to him. He knows what he's talking about," said Peter.

"Do you know Lord Deverill well?" asked Cassandra on a sudden impulse.

Peter hesitated. "We're . . . acquainted," he said.

"He, too, was a friend of Rupert's."

"Really?"

"Yes. Or at least they knew each other. Perhaps theirs was only an acquaintance, too."

"Perhaps so."

He was not being very helpful and she felt that she had taken up enough of his time. He was probably longing for her to go so that he could ask some young lady to dance. Either that, or retire to the card-room, where he could spend the evening gambling.

"As long as Mr. Goddard feels it was nothing important, then I think I can set my mind at rest," said Cassandra. "He is not in town at the moment, Lord Deverill says. Do you know when he'll be back?"

"Soon. He's never away for very long. I shouldn't wonder if he was back by the end of the week."

"Do you know where he lives?" she persisted.

Peter shook his head.

"He moves about. He doesn't have a house here—he can't afford it. He gambled away his inheritance, so he has to take lodgings, but you can find him at the races. He always goes, whenever he's in Brighton. It's one of his favourite haunts."

"Then I must hope to speak to him there. Thank you, it was kind of you to speak to me."

"A pleasure," he said, making her a bow.

Cassandra returned to Maria and Harry. Now that her conversation with Peter was over she felt she could enjoy the ball. She felt her spirits lift. The room was colourful and the music lively. It was a long time since she had had so much fun.

She was just hoping that Harry would ask her to dance with him again when Captain Wade came up to her, bringing Lord Deverill with him. He was dressed in restrained style, but his coat showed the mark of the best London tailoring.

"May I say what pleasure it gave me to see two such fine dancers enjoying themselves at the Castle?" said Captain Wade genially, as he smiled at Cassandra and Harry. "The rooms were graced by your cotillion. It is always pleasing to see people enjoying themselves in such a manner."

Lord Deverill smiled at Captain Wade's flowery speech, then set his face along more sober lines as Captain Wade turned towards him.

"Lord Deverill, might I present Miss Paxton, and her friends, Mr. and Mrs. Winter?" he asked.

We've already met, Cassandra was about to say, when she realized that it had not been a formal introduction, and that such an admission might provoke awkward questions.

"Charmed," said Lord Deverill, inclining his head. "Miss Paxton, would you do me the honour of dancing with me?"

Cassandra agreed, then, ignoring Maria's wide smile, she took Lord Deverill's arm. As she did so, she felt a frisson of awareness travel through her, but before she could wonder what it was they had taken their places on the floor and positioned themselves opposite each other. The musicians struck the opening chords and the dance began.

"I did not expect to see you here this evening," she said.

"No?"

"You didn't mention that you would be coming when I spoke to you earlier."

"I didn't know. I had some business to attend to, and I didn't know how long it would take me. But I like to look in on the assemblies when I have time. You have satisfied yourself with regard to your brother, I hope? I saw you speaking to Peter Raistrick."

"Yes. He felt as you do, that I have nothing to be concerned about."

"Good." They swapped partners, then came back together again. "Do you intend to stay in Brighton long?" he asked.

"I will be here for most of the summer, I think."

"Then I hope you will enjoy your few weeks' holiday. When was the last time you were here?"

"Four years ago," she said, thinking that the last time she had visited Brighton, she had done so with her family.

"You will find it has changed."

"Yes." She became wistful. "Everything changes."

"What do you intend to do whilst you are here?" he asked.

"I mean to go sea bathing, and go to the races," she said, rousing herself. "Mr. Raistrick tells me I will find Mr. Goddard there."

"Very likely," said Lord Deverill drily. "Have you been before?"

"Yes, I went with my family. Rupert was always fond of a wager, and my mother loved the course. She said it was the prettiest one in England."

"It probably is," he said. "Whitehawk Down's a beautiful place in its own right, and of course it overlooks the sea. On a clear day the views are spectacular."

"My father always claimed that if the weather was good he could see all the way to France." She sighed. "It is a pity about France. I have always wanted to go there, but now that the Peace of Amiens has broken down it is too dangerous to go. Have you ever been?"

"Yes, I went as a child, before the Revolution, and I went to Paris again during the peace. It is a city worth seeing."

They talked of the latest books and plays, of the delights of the country and the joys of the seaside, and the dance passed very quickly. As the final chords sounded, Cassandra was surprised how enjoyable it had been. There had been none of the constraint she had noticed when she had called at his house, but then of course, this time he had been prepared for the meeting.

"Cassie, Lord Deverill's notice has made you," said Maria as Cassandra joined her at the side of the room. "Look, here is Captain Wade coming towards you again, and he is bringing Lord Armington."

Maria was right. Captain Wade performed the introductions, and before she knew it, Cassandra found herself being led out on to the floor again.

Lord Armington was an elegant man who danced with grace. As she partnered him, she found that she was entertained by his knowledgeable conversation. He told her of his art collections and his books, and the museum he meant to set up in his grounds.

"I knew how it would be," said Maria, when the dance came to an end. "You only had to be seen to be noticed. Lord Armington would make a splendid catch. He has an old name and a huge fortune. He's a connoisseur of beauty, and I should not be surprised if he offers for you before the month is out."

"Really, Maria," said Cassandra, laughing. "He can't be expected to marry every young lady he partners."

"Which is why he seldom dances. But he has broken with his own tradition in order to dance with you," said Maria.

Harry coughed. "I believe he's just asked Miss Lumax to dance."

Cassandra and Harry exchanged humorous glances. Maria, however, dismissed it regally.

"I dare say he did it so he would not look particular for dancing with Cassie," she said.

There were no more dancers heading for the floor as it was time for supper. A number of people were already leaving the ballroom. Harry was about to offer each lady an arm when Cassandra saw that Lord Deverill was heading towards them again.

"Miss Paxton, would you do me the honour of going into supper with me?" he asked.

"Thank you, I would."

Together they joined the crowd of people heading for the supper room and took their places at the supper table. Lord Deverill sat on her right, next to a beauty with dusky curls who smiled up at him and greeted him warmly. The beauty then flashed a look of loathing at Cassandra, and her mother did likewise.

If they only knew he has no interest in me, and that he is just being polite to a sister of one of his friends, thought Cassandra with amusement.

The young beauty monopolized Lord Deverill's attention and Cassandra turned to her left. She expected to find Harry there, but a number of other couples had come between them, so that Maria and Harry had had to take their places further down the table. Instead, she found she was sitting next to a well-dressed gentleman with curly brown hair. She inclined her head, and he made her a slight bow. She allowed her gaze to wander round the supper-room. It was an elegant apartment, and the food that was beginning to be served was tempting.

Escaping the attentions of the dusky beauty, Lord Deverill asked her what she would have. She chose chicken in aspic, hot lobster and oyster pâté, whilst he took a helping of turtle. She was about to ask him whether he would be at the races later in the week when his attention was claimed by a pretty blonde young lady on the other side of the table.

Cassandra smiled ruefully and took a mouthful of chicken. It seemed she was not going to have an opportunity to speak to him further, despite sitting next to him.

She was rescued from her silence by the gentlemen to her left.

"It's a pleasure to see you here," he said.

He dabbed his mouth fastidiously with his napkin.

"I don't believe we've met," she said, putting her fork down in surprise.

"No, we haven't. A sad mistake, but one I am repairing." He smiled charmingly. "Allow me to introduce myself. My name is Elwin. I knew your brother," he said.

"Ah."

She should have expected it. Rupert must have had many more friends than Mr. Raistrick and Mr. Goddard.

"I'm very pleased to make your acquaintance," she said.

"And I yours. I did not expect to see you in Brighton. You have not visited for some time."

"No," she said, a little sadly.

"Forgive me. That was tactless. You have been in mourning. But I am glad to see you here now. Have you had an opportunity to do very much since you arrived?"

"No, very little. I've only been here for a few days."

"There is so much to see and do, and it changes all the time. I know you visited regularly when you were younger—Rupert spoke of you often," he said. "But you will find it different to your last visit. There is a lot of building taking place, and the Prince is carrying out more work on his Pavilion. Have you seen it?"

"Yes, I have. It was one of the first things I saw when I arrived. The stables look rather strange," said Cassandra.

"They do indeed. They look like something out of an Oriental dream. But they are nothing to the inside. You must make sure you see it." He took a sip of wine. "The poor Prince has nothing to do, of course, and is bored. That is why he is forever altering things.

He told her many tales about the Prince, some of them risqué, but all of them amusing. As supper wore on, and grape pudding, ices, soufflés, and little cakes soaked in rum replaced the chicken and turtle, the conversation moved to Cassandra, and she revealed that she had come to Brighton to prepare her house for sale.

"Oh, but surely that isn't necessary," said Mr. Elwin.

"Unfortunately it is," she said.

"There must be another solution to the problem, especially for someone of your beauty," said Mr. Elwin.

"You flatter me," she said.

"Not at all. Any looking-glass will tell you you are uncommonly beautiful."

"It doesn't prevent me from being poor, alas," she said, turning the compliment aside.

"Of course it does. You can make a fortune from your face and figure. Only say the word, and I'll introduce you to a number of wealthy gentlemen."

"Thank you, but I have no plans to marry."

He took a drink of wine.

"I wasn't talking about marriage. Without a dowry you'll find it difficult to make a respectable match, especially as you have no influential friends to help you, but marriage isn't the only option. Brighton is a tolerant town and there are other, more exciting, avenues to explore. Many of the gentlemen of my acquaintance would be pleased to give you anything you wanted. In fact, they would offer you carte blanche."

Cassandra could not believe what she was hearing. *Carte blanche?* Anything she pleased—if she was prepared to sell herself? She was astonished he had the audacity to suggest it—and then she felt herself growing angry. If she had been anywhere but at the supper table she would have walked away, but she was trapped.

"You insult me," she said sharply.

He drank the rest of his wine, then dabbed his mouth fastidiously again.

"Not at all. It's a great compliment. The gentlemen I am thinking of can have their choice of female companions, from the wittiest to the most beautiful. You should be honoured they might choose you."

"I think you had better say no more," returned Cassandra, putting down her fork with a clatter.

"Why so superior?" he asked mockingly. "Rupert was never above his company."

"I can't think he would have wanted you to insult his sister in this way," she returned.

Mr. Elwin laughed. "He'd have been trying to persuade you as much as I am. He was always fond of money."

Cassandra was so disgusted she half rose from her seat. Lord Deverill looked up at her in surprise, his attention caught, and further along the table she saw Maria look startled. She sat down again, determined not to let Mr. Elwin provoke her. It would not do to make a scene, but she was sorely tried. Fortunately for her self control, supper was almost at an end, and she would only have to endure Mr. Elwin's company for a few minutes more.

"Think over what I've said," Mr. Elwin told her, as the guests began to leave the table. "You could have your house paid for, and a neat little carriage, with a couple of high steppers to pull it. Clothes, jewels . . . everything you want could be yours."

Cassandra did not deign to reply. The supper party was breaking up. Leaving the table quickly, she walked out of the room, determined to escape before Lord Deverill or Maria could ask her what was wrong. She was so angry she could not rely on herself to make a sensible reply. She headed for the ladies' withdrawing room so that she could have a few minutes to calm herself before returning to the ballroom.

She had not gone far, however, when she realized she was lost. The corridors all looked the same. But she did not need to find the withdrawing room. Any empty chamber would do. She hesitated. To her left was a row of doors. Listening outside the first, she satisfied herself that it was empty and then went in. It was dim inside. The candles were not lit, and the only illumination came from the fading daylight. There were a few comfortable chairs and a card table set in front of an empty grate. She ignored them and walked over to the window, then stood looking out into the twilight. She breathed in deeply. The unpleasant encounter had shaken her more than she cared to admit. She had originally thought of asking Mr. Elwin about her brother's letter, but now she was determined never to speak to him again.

By and by she felt herself growing calm. She turned away from the window, knowing she must return to the ballroom before she was missed, but just as she was about to return to the company she saw the door handle turn. She looked around but there was nowhere to hide. She braced herself for the startled look of whoever was about to enter the room, then the door opened and she saw the last person she wanted to see.

It was Lord Deverill.

CHAPTER THREE

"Lord Deverill," she exclaimed in surprise. "What are you doing here?"

"You left the supper room very quickly," he said, looking at her intently. "I wondered whether anything was the matter?"

"No," she said hurriedly. "Nothing at all."

He did not immediately reply, but by the way he was looking at her she could tell that he did not believe her. Then he said, "I wondered if Elwin had said anything to upset you."

"Of course not. What could he possibly say that would upset me?"

She spoke with a show of bravado, but she was becoming increasingly aware of the fact that he was not deceived. She did not want to tell him what Mr. Elwin had said, however, because it was too humiliating.

"I don't know," he replied. "That's what I am asking you."

"He didn't say anything," she said defiantly.

"In that case, why did you stand up in the middle of supper?"

"Did I?" she prevaricated.

"Yes. You did. You flushed, then looked angry, then half rose from your seat, as though you meant to walk out of the room."

"You must be mistaken. You were busy talking to the other guests and you must have misunderstood."

"Then why are you wringing your hands?"

"I'm—" She was about to say, *I'm not*, when looking down, she realized she was doing just that.

"Why did you stand up?" he asked again.

"I . . . I have been here too long. I must return to the ballroom, or else Maria will be wondering where I am," she said.

She walked towards him but he did not move aside and she was forced to step round him, brushing against him as she passed. The contact was unnerving enough, but it was far worse when his hand caught her wrist in a vice-like grip.

"You're not going anywhere until you've told me what Elwin said."

She was suddenly aware of how large he was. He seemed to have grown so that he almost filled the room.

"Let go," she said, feeling her pulse start to race. "You're hurting me." She wrenched her hand away from him.

"I'm trying to help you," he said through gritted teeth. "Your brother had some dubious friends, Cassandra, and you'd be wise to keep away from them. Now tell me, what did Elwin say?"

"Let me pass," she said defiantly, raising her head.

"No," he returned sharply.

"Do you mean to keep me a prisoner here?" she demanded.

"If necessary, yes."

She looked him in the eye, startled, and saw that he was serious.

"This is abominable," she said.

"If Elwin said nothing wrong, then you won't mind telling me what it was," he remarked steadily.

"It was nothing," she said, throwing him off. "He told me about the Prince of Wales and his secret marriage, his building plans, and—"

"The truth."

He folded his arms, which gave him an even bulkier shape in the twilight, and his large body cast dark shadows on the floor.

Cassandra turned away from him and walked over to the mantelpiece, gathering her thoughts. She straightened the clock and fiddled with a candlestick, unwilling to speak, and yet knowing that he would not let her go if she did not. She heard a slight sound of movement and felt him approaching her until she knew he was standing behind her.

"He has said something to upset you," he said, more gently. "I tried to warn you. I told you that not all of Rupert's friends were respectable. I didn't want you to be hurt. What did he say?"

"He said . . ." She turned to face him. "He said that he would introduce me to some gentlemen who would . . . who would . . ."

"Yes?"

She bit her lips, then said, ". . . who would offer me carte blanche."

"Ah. I see."

He didn't seem surprised. In fact, he seemed relieved. His calm acceptance of it stung her.

"You see nothing wrong in that?" she demanded.

"I see everything wrong in it," he said.

"But you were expecting worse—though what could be worse, I can't imagine."

Even as she said it, her imagination took flight. Perhaps Lord Deverill had suspected that Mr. Elwin would suggest she be passed between gentlemen, instead of being the favoured mistress of one or other of them. She shuddered.

"Keep away from Elwin," he said. "If Rupert was here, he would say the same. Elwin is not the sort of man you should know."

"So I have discovered, but have no fear. I never intend to talk to him again."

Lord Deverill nodded slightly, then said, "It's possible he might approach you. If he does, I want you to know that you can call on me for help at any time."

There was something gentle in his tone of voice, and she felt herself relax as the tension started to ebb.

"That's very kind of you," she said, "but it isn't your concern."

"That's where you're wrong. It is."

She looked at him enquiringly.

He indicated a chair. She hesitated, and then sat down, curious to know what he meant.

He picked up a tinderbox and lit the candles on the mantelpiece. The small yellow flames flickered into life. As they gained strength they created soft pools of light that glowed in the twilight. He replaced the tinder box and then sat down opposite her. He stretched his legs out in front of him. Light gleamed from the gold ring on his finger, and the diamond pin in his cravat. But it was his eyes that drew Cassandra's attention, and the finger that stroked his top lip.

He started speaking.

"Your brother made me promise him something, last year, when he lay dying." He spoke heavily, as though the recollection was not pleasant. "That is why I say it is my concern if you are worried or in difficulties."

Cassandra was puzzled.

"What kind of promise? And why were you with him when he lay dying? I thought he was riding alone. Were you with him when he fell?"

"Yes. I was."

His eyes suddenly flickered and dropped to the floor. She had the feeling that he was not seeing her, but that he was seeing the past, reliving the moment when Rupert had been thrown from his horse.

"Did . . . did he suffer?" she asked in a low voice.

"No. He felt nothing."

"And . . . and the end?" asked Cassandra, with a catch in her throat.

He spoke gently. "Was very quick."

"I have often . . ." She stopped to collect herself, then began again in a stronger voice. "I have often wondered about that night. I asked Mr. Raistrick about it, but he could tell me nothing. Why was Rupert riding at night? What was he doing? Where was he going? Why was he ignoring the safety of his horse? Was he drunk? Was that the explanation?"

"No, he wasn't drunk," he said slowly.

"Then what made him ride across rough country in the dark? Did he do it for a bet? To try and set a record for racing from Brighton to London overnight, perhaps?"

He regarded her intently for a moment, and then said, "It's impossible to be sure."

"If the bet was sufficiently large, he might have been tempted to risk his horse," she said, following her own train of thought. "He had always wanted to find a quick and easy way of repairing the family fortunes, even from the time he was a small boy." She smiled sadly as she recalled a childhood memory, and began to pleat the skirt of her gown. "When he was eleven years old, he came across an old family journal in the library, written by my great great great great grandfather. It mentioned that my ancestor had buried the family jewels under a chestnut tree before fleeing to France after the Civil War. Rupert took a spade outside and started digging up one of the chestnut trees! The only way my father could stop him was to show him another journal which he kept in the study. It told of the family's subsequent uprooting of every chestnut on the estate after their return from France, and their failure to find the treasure." Her mouth quirked. "My ancestor had had expensive habits, including a very expensive mistress, and my father suspected he had given the jewels to her, claiming to have buried them when the rest of the family asked where they were!

But Rupert still dreamed of it, and invented a game of buried treasure: on wet afternoons, he would dream of all the things he would buy if the family jewels were ever found. Winning a large bet would be akin to finding buried treasure."

She fell silent, thinking of her brother. At last she roused herself.

"You said you made my brother a promise?"

"Yes." He lifted his eyes to hers. "When I went over to him, it was clear he was dying. He told me that he had two sisters who would be left without any male relative to help them in case of need. He wanted me to promise that I would help you if ever you needed it."

"But why?" asked Cassandra. "I did not know that the two of you were on such good terms."

She caught a flash of something in his eye, a curious mixture of pain and anger and regret, but then it was gone, and she was left with the feeling that she must have imagined it.

"I—" he began.

He broke off as a door opened further down the corridor, and the sound of voices could be heard. The voices grew louder, approaching the door.

Cassandra froze. She was alone in a dimly lit ante-room with a gentleman. If she was discovered, her reputation would be ruined. She sprang from her chair. The voices grew louder . . . and then passed. It had been a narrow escape, but she could not afford to stay there any longer. She had been foolish to remain for so long.

"I must return to the ballroom," she said, knowing that every minute increased the chance of discovery.

He nodded. "You will call on me if you need any help?" he asked. "You know where I live. A note will bring me to you at any time."

"Yes. I will. Thank you. But I don't expect I will see Mr. Elwin again."

She went over to the door and listened. Everything was quiet. She opened it cautiously and looked out. The corridor was empty. She slipped out of the room and made her way back to the ballroom, drawn by the sound of music.

The ballroom seemed dazzling. After the dimness of the ante-room, she found the light almost painful. The noise, too, troubled her. She was no longer in the mood for frivolity, and wanted to go home. She could not escape her duty, however, and when Captain Wade introduced her to a new partner she was forced to take his hand and go on to the dance floor.

The gentleman in question was a foppish young man, dressed in a tight coat and breeches, by the name of Mr. Kingsley. Yellow stockings adorned his legs, and his hair was elaborately curled. His conversation revolved around clothes, canes and snuff boxes, and to begin with, Cassandra found it irritating. By and by, however, she began to emerge from her dark thoughts and return to the light, so that she was able to take an interest in the conversation. It ended with her agreeing that lace fans were more elegant than chicken skin, and that every well-dressed gentleman should be in possession of a silver-topped cane.

"What an enjoyable evening!" said Maria, as they met again at the side of the floor. "I missed you after supper, but then I saw you dancing with Mr. Kingsley and knew you must be enjoying yourself. He is rather ridiculous, but he is a dear." She looked around. "The evening is drawing to an end. It's time for us to go. Where's Harry? Ah, there he is." She caught Harry's attention. "It's time to go home," she told him.

"I was just thinking the same thing myself."

The ladies collected their shawls and then waited for the carriage to be brought round. Harry helped them in and they were on their way. As the coach pulled away, Cassandra saw Lord Deverill leaving the assembly rooms and mounting his horse. Their eyes met for a moment, and held. He was a perplexing man. He was polite on the surface, at times even charming, but there was something disturbing underneath.

Then the coach turned a corner and he was lost from view.

"I have had a wonderful time," said Maria. "We must do it again."

"Yes, it was very . . . interesting," said Cassandra, recalling her thoughts.

"Now, don't forget we are going bathing in the morning," said Maria, as the carriage rolled to a halt outside Cassandra's house.

"No, I won't. I'm looking forward to it," said Cassandra as she climbed out of the carriage.

"I will call for you at ten o'clock."

They said their farewells, then the carriage rolled away.

Cassandra went indoors. She was tired after the evening's events, and was looking forward to retreating to the peace and quiet of her room.

"Out all hours. You'll be fit for nothing in the morning, I'll be bound," said Moll, greeting her with gruff affection. "Did you enjoy yourself?"

"Yes," said Cassandra with a tired smile. "I did."

She said nothing to Moll about some of the more disturbing aspects of her evening. Indeed, she did not want to think of them herself.

"About time you had some frolics," said Moll approvingly. "Did all the gennulmen dance with you?"

"Not all of them," Cassandra teased her. "But I danced every dance."

"Ah." Moll nodded in satisfaction. "I knew how it would be."

Cassandra yawned.

"You'll be tired," said Moll. "I've put a hot brick in your bed. It's come colder this evening."

Cassandra went upstairs. She sat down in front of the dressing table and unclasped the simple string of pearls from around her neck, laying it in its box. Then she pulled off her gloves and unpinned her hair. She stood up so that Moll could unfasten her gown and then stepped out of it. Corset, chemise and drawers followed, and Moll helped her into her lawn nightdress.

As Cassandra fastened the nightdress, pulling the drawstring at the neck, she found her thoughts returning to Lord Deverill. What had been the meaning of the look he had given her as she had left the assembly rooms behind? What did he know of Mr. Elwin?

And why had he been with her brother on the night he died?

CHAPTER FOUR

The following morning dawned bright and fair. Cassandra woke at five o'clock, with the sun streaming in at her window. She was used to country hours and, despite her late night at the assembly rooms, she had no desire to stay in bed. She rose, washed and dressed, and then went downstairs. Moll brought her a breakfast of chocolate and hot rolls and she ate it by the open window in the parlour. When she had finished she looked at the clock. She had almost four hours before Maria called for her, and she meant to put the time to good use. She had a lot to do if she wanted to prepare the house for sale.

"I thought we would make a start on the attic today," she said to Moll. "It will have to be cleaned at some time."

"You should hire some more servants, Miss Cassie," grumbled Moll. "It's more than the two of us can see to."

"You know there's no spare money for servants. It has taken nearly everything we have just to come here. But we will manage."

She and Moll went down to the kitchen, where Cassandra put on an apron, then they both collected buckets and cloths and went up to the attic. Cassandra stopped on the landing at the top. The attic was split into four rooms, and a glance through each of the doors showed that the rooms were filled with broken furniture, old trunks and sundry items that did not belong anywhere else. The rooms were all very dusty, and they smelt stale.

"We'll start in here, I think."

She went into the first room and opened the window wide. A fresh smell invaded the room. She breathed in deeply, thinking that the freshness was one of the things she loved most about Brighton, particularly in the summer, and that it was one of the things she would miss most. She heard the call of the gulls and the rush of the sea, and leaning out of the window, she managed to glimpse the water. How she loved it! And how she would miss it. She was conscious of a sinking of her spirits. To be forced to sell the town house, which had been such a large part of her life as a child, was a great sadness. Her summer holidays as well as the grey winter months had been enlivened by trips to the seaside and had varied the domestic scene. And now, soon, it would be a thing of the past. . . . But she had had it for many years, she consoled herself, and had been the richer for it.

Did she really have to sell it? she wondered. If she could bring herself to marry for money and position, then she could keep it, and both she and Lizzie would have it for years to come. The idea was tempting, and the thought of Lord Armington came to mind. A moment later she laughed at herself. As if Lord Armington would propose marriage! She was becoming as fanciful as Maria! But it was possible some gentleman might propose. Could she do it? Could she accept? It would make her life far easier. But to live, every day, with a man she did not love—to sit with him at table, eat with him . . . no, it was not to be borne. She would sell the house, and she and Lizzie would spend the rest of their lives in the country.

"Soonest started, soonest finished," grumbled Moll, bringing her thoughts back to the present.

They were soon hard at work. Cassandra sorted through the discarded and broken furniture, reflecting that Rupert had spent more on one cabinet than she and Lizzie had spent in a whole year. She sighed at the thought of her brother's profligate ways, but then turned her thoughts to more practical concerns, deciding if any of the furniture would be of use on the estate. Some of it was of good quality and would fit in well in the country, so she set it to one side. Anything that was broken she put on the landing, shuffling it there with Moll's help.

"John can take the pieces I am keeping to the estate in the coach, once it has been repaired," she said. "The rest he can dispose of."

Having sorted through the furniture, she helped Moll with the cleaning. The sun rose in the sky. At last, tired, she sat back on her heels and pushed her hair out of her face. It had come loose of its chignon, and was falling in golden strands around her neck.

"I just hopes all this work is worth it," said Moll darkly. "There might not be anyone looking for a town house."

"Someone is sure to want it," said Cassandra. "Now that the Prince of Wales has made his home in Brighton it's become popular with all the most fashionable people, and it's easy to see why. There is so much for them to do. There are the balls and assemblies, the races and the bathing . . ." She glanced at the clock on the mantelpiece, whose hands showed that it was half past nine. She threw down her duster. "Maria will be here soon. I had better go and change into something more suitable."

"All this sea bathing. I don't hold with it," said Moll. "You'll catch your death," she predicted dourly.

"I don't suppose it will be as bad as that. I will probably only contract pneumonia," said Cassandra teasingly.

"And who'll have to nurse you if you do, that's what I want to know?"

"You'll enjoy it," Cassandra said humorously. "You know you always love looking after me. Now, I will need a towel, and a dry chemise to change into when I have bathed."

Muttering under her breath, Moll went to fetch them. Cassandra removed her apron and tidied her hair, and then ran over to the window as she heard a carriage pulling up outside. It was Maria. She went downstairs with Moll behind her, and putting on her spencer and bonnet she went outside.

"I've sent James away," said Maria. "It's such a lovely morning, I thought we would walk."

"A good idea," said Cassandra, feeling the warmth of the sun on her face and thinking that a walk would be just the thing.

She and Maria unfurled their parasols and strolled down to the beach. Moll grumbled along behind them. Despite the early hour, they were not the only promenaders. A number of other ladies and gentlemen were strolling along, taking the air. A young boy propelled himself along on a pedestrian curricle, dodging in and out of them, and a dog ran along behind him, barking. Urchins followed the dog, trying to catch it, and a baker ran along behind the urchins, shaking his fist as one of them crammed chunks of a stolen loaf into his mouth. A buxom young maid called out the virtues of her pastries, and a footman ran out into the road, intent on hailing a hackney carriage for his mistress.

Cassandra and Maria walked on to the beach, with Moll still complaining behind them. Cassandra's eye wandered over the brightly coloured bathing machines. The wooden huts rested on the top of four large iron wheels which were red with rust. Some of them were already in use, standing in the water, and one of them was in the act of being drawn in to the sea. It was being pulled by a heavy horse, who was being urged on by a ragged urchin perched on its back.

Cassandra and Maria approached the nearest machine and arranged to take it, then climbed up the steps that led inside. Moll followed them, puffing and panting as she climbed the steps.

"Like a gypsy caravan," grumbled Moll. "Not fit for a decent body."

"It's not so very bad," said Cassandra. "In fact, it's very clean, much better than the one I had last time."

The machine was not only clean, it was spacious inside. A wooden seat ran down both sides of it, and in the middle of it there was a clear space, ideal for undressing. Cassandra and Maria took off their gowns, with Moll's help, and then removed their corsets. They sat on the seat and took off their satin shoes, then rolled off their stockings. At last, dressed in nothing but their chemises, they declared themselves ready.

"I tried to persuade Harry to bathe as well, but he said if he wanted to kill himself he'd do it in a civilized way, with brandy and cigars, instead of catching his death in the water," said Maria with a sigh. "It's a pity, because I'm sure he'd enjoy it. The gentlemen's part of the beach is always busy."

There was a bump and the machine began to move. It crunched over the beach and then swished and sloshed as it entered the water. When it was deep enough, the urchin halted the horse and Cassandra descended the steps, with Maria behind her. She gasped as she felt the sea creeping over her feet, then her knees, then her thighs.

"It's cold!" she exclaimed.

At the bottom of the steps there was a dipper, a jovial fat woman dressed in a shapeless garment like an enveloping nightgown, with a cap on her head. She helped Cassandra down the last few remaining steps and dipped her into the water.

"It's a lovely day for it," the dipper said.

Cassandra agreed. She was becoming used to the temperature, and as soon as she was immersed she struck out to sea, away from the bottom of the steps.

Maria launched herself forward and swam a few ungainly strokes.

"I wish Mama had taught me to swim as a child," she said. "I used to see you in the water with your mother and envy you, but Mama said it was undignified."

"Perhaps it is," said Cassandra. "But it's also great fun."

They swam on together, then stopped to talk.

"Look at all the beautiful bathing dresses," said Cassandra.

Whilst some of the ladies were bathing in their petticoats, others were dressed in colourful garments that were as well designed as ball gowns. An elegant young lady swam past, and Cassandra recognized the dusky-haired beauty from the assembly rooms.

"That's Miss Kerrith," said Maria. "I've told you about her before. She's set her cap at Lord Deverill, and means to have him if she can. I think she will succeed. His father speculated unwisely and lost the family fortune, and he needs to marry an heiress."

Cassandra continued to watch Miss Kerrith. The young beauty's bathing dress was a delicate shade of pink, and was adorned with ribbon roses. It clung to her perfect form in the water, showing every curve. Her bathing cap was designed to match, and covered all but the front row of her dusky curls.

"She is always exquisitely dressed," said Maria. "I'm tempted to buy a bathing gown myself, but it seems such a waste. The salt water will quickly ruin it, and besides, there is no one of any importance to see it."

Although some of the bathers were young, many were elderly or infirm. Cassandra and Maria moved away from them and began to swim again. Cassandra soon outstripped Maria. She turned on her back and floated along in the sunshine. She was just about to turn on to her front again and swim back to Maria when a flailing arm hit her across the throat and she was knocked under the water. Unfortunately, not all of the ladies who took to the water could swim, and such incidents were not uncommon. She righted herself, and was just about to turn round and offer her assistance when another whirling arm pushed her under again. She surfaced and tried to help, but she was hit again by whirling arms and legs. She was pushed under the water, and by some unlucky chance, the arms and legs kept her under. She struggled to reach the surface, but when she was kicked again she decided to escape the flailing limbs by swimming along underwater. When she had gone far enough to be safe, she emerged from the waves and gulped down precious lungfuls of air. She was wiping the water out of her eyes when Maria swam up beside her.

"What happened?" asked Maria in concern.

"One of the women needed help," said Cassandra. "I tried to give it to her, but she kept pushing me under the water. There's always someone in trouble. Most of the women here only swim when they're on holiday. They go along quite contentedly, then suddenly they find they are out of their depth and start to panic."

"Where did it happen?" asked Maria.

Cassandra looked round, but there was no sign of any windmilling arms and legs, and no splashes or sounds of anyone in distress. The ladies nearby were swimming along serenely, or standing up to their waists in the water and gossiping.

"One of the dippers must have helped her, or she must have managed to find her feet."

"As long as she doesn't come near me," said Maria anxiously. "I'm not very confident in the water, and I don't want anyone pulling me under the waves."

Despite her words, Maria was reasonably proficient, and she and Cassandra swam on together, enjoying the freshness of the water and the sound of the surf in their ears.

As time passed they began to grow cold and at last they were ready to go home. They returned to their bathing machine and climbed the steps. Water streamed from their chemises and poured from their hair.

"You'll catch your deaths, just see if you don't," grumbled Moll as she wrapped them in towels.

Cassandra and Maria exchanged glances and smiled, then gave their attention to dressing. Before long they were ready to go.

"A hot bath, that's what you'll need when we get home," said Moll as the three of them left the bathing hut.

They began to walk up the beach. As they did so, Cassandra caught sight of a figure she recognized. It was Lord Deverill. He saw them and greeted them, making a bow.

"I see you have been bathing," he said. "It is very intrepid of you."

"There's nothing nicer on a fine day," said Cassandra.

"Are you returning home?"

"Yes."

"Then allow me to escort you."

He offered her his arm. She hesitated, remembering the strange frisson that had assailed her when she had taken his arm at the ball, but then, not wishing to appear particular, she put her hand lightly on his arm. Again, she felt a shiver of awareness wash over her.

He appeared not to notice it. He offered Maria his other arm, but she claimed she wanted to speak to Moll and fell behind them.

"Do you swim?" Cassandra asked him.

"Yes, I do. It's one of the things I enjoy most about living in Brighton."

"Have you always lived here?"

"No. I grew up on a country estate, but my father had to sell it when I was at Oxford. Since leaving, I have lived here."

Cassandra found her thoughts wandering back to their previous conversation.

"When I spoke to you at the assembly rooms, you said you had promised Rupert you would help me if I ever needed it. I knew that you and he were friends because I had overheard him talking about you, but I did not know you were on such intimate terms. Did you know each other well?"

"Well enough," he said non-committally.

"I'm surprised he did not tell me all about you. He was always dazzled by titles."

"Whereas you are not," he said, turning to look at her.

"I like them well enough. But they are like the ribbon on a gown. A fine ribbon will improve even the most beautiful dress, but it will not disguise a poor fit or shoddy stitching."

He laughed. "It's the first time I've ever been compared to a gown!" He glanced at her. "I hope I am not shoddily made?"

"Not at all. You are—" She had been going to say, You are very well made, but stopped herself just in time, saying instead, "a very good man, I am sure. You must be, if you promised to help the sisters of an acquaintance. Even so, I'm surprised Rupert asked you. I would have expected him to ask Mr. Raistrick, perhaps, or Mr. Goddard."

"I was the only person with him when he died," he said. "He had no one else to ask."

Her mood sobered. "I wish Rupert had not been so wild. If he had not gone riding at night, he would still be alive today."

They crossed the road, threading their way through carts and carriages, and arrived safely at the other side.

"Why were you with Rupert that night?" asked Cassandra.

"I often go out riding on the Downs. Do you mean to ride now you are in Brighton?" he asked, changing the subject.

"No. Ever since Rupert's accident, I just don't want to ride any more."

"You should have climbed on a horse straight away," he said.

"I did. I made sure Lizzie did, too. She had always loved riding, but she did not want to go once Rupert had fallen. So I encouraged her, and she overcame her fear."

"But you did not overcome yours?"

"I overcame the fear, but the joy of riding did not come back."

"Perhaps, in time, it will."

"Perhaps."

They reached the door.

"Thank you. It was very kind of you to escort us."

"Not at all."

He bowed over her hand and kissed it. She felt a strange sensation, a hot tingle, and her eyes were drawn to his. She saw a flash of something unrecognizable but strangely compelling there, and then it was gone.

Maria and Moll joined them.

"You must come to my soirée," said Maria as Lord Deverill made her a bow. "I am holding it next week."

Cassandra expected him to make a polite excuse, but instead he said, "I'd be delighted."

Maria glowed. Cassandra found that she was glad yet unsettled at the same time. He made his farewells and then walked away.

"You seem to have found a guardian angel, Cassie," said Maria.

"Nonsense," said Cassandra. "Lord Deverill just happened to be passing when we left the beach."

"Perhaps," said Maria.

They went inside.

It had been agreed that Maria would stay with Cassandra for the rest of the day. Harry was engaged in business and would collect Maria on his way home after dinner.

"A hot bath, now," said Moll as she disappeared into the kitchen.

Cassandra and Maria followed her. If she had been able to afford a houseful of servants, Cassandra would have liked nothing better than to bathe in her dressing-room, but as it was, she did not want Moll to have to carry heavy cans of hot water upstairs.

As she helped Moll pull the hip bath out into the middle of the kitchen floor, she thought over what Maria had said. Was Lord Deverill her guardian angel? Was he watching over her? Perhaps he felt he owed it to her brother.

She and Maria took it in turns to bathe, then went to sit outside. The sun was still shining, and the small area behind the house was not overlooked. It was in a quiet alley, unfrequented by fashionable people and rarely traversed by servants. She and Maria arranged their hair across their shoulders and settled down for a comfortable gossip.

"I was thinking," said Cassandra, "that I would like to go to the races."

"Oh, what a good idea," said Maria. "I think you'll find Mr. Kingsley will be there, too." She saw Cassandra's face. "Don't look at me like that, Cassie. I saw you dancing with him last night and he looked very taken with you. He's not as good a catch as Lord Armington, of course, but it does no harm to have more than one suitor. He's very wealthy, and he really is rather a dear."

"He danced with me. He didn't offer me marriage," Cassandra said.

"Oh, Cassie, I do wish you'd make more of your chances.

If you married, you could keep the town house and you could holiday here every summer. Wouldn't you like that?"

Cassandra hesitated. Her visit to Brighton had been full of surprising incidents: her meeting with Mr. Elwin, her encounters with Lord Deverill and her ducking in the water. It wasn't quite the restful place she remembered.

"Of course you would," said Maria, answering the question for her.

Moll brought them both a cup of tea, "To stop you catching your deaths," she said, and they drank the refreshing brew.

"I invited Mr. Kingsley to my soirée," Maria continued, "but he had another engagement." She put her cup down in her saucer. "Never mind, Lord Armington has accepted. And what a lucky chance it was that I could also invite Lord Deverill."

"Lord Deverill needs to marry an heiress," Cassandra reminded her, putting her cup down.

"That is so, but it will do Lord Armington no harm to have a rival."

"It's very kind of you, Maria, and I do appreciate everything you are trying to do for me," said Cassandra, turning to face her, "but I wish you would not encourage me to see every man as a husband."

"Not every man," said Maria. "Just the eligible ones."

Cassandra laughed and shook her head.

"Don't set your mind against it too soon," said Maria,

unperturbed. "When you come to know one of the gentlemen better, then you might change your mind."

~ ~ ~

Justin returned home.

"There is a person to see you, my lord," said Manby, as he entered the house.

"A person?" said Justin, turning to look at his butler.

"Yes, my lord," said Manby. "I have put him in the library."

Justin went through into the library, where a roughly dressed man was waiting for him.

"So you got my message," said Justin.

"Yes, m'lord. There's something you want doing?"

"There is. I want someone watching. A Miss Paxton." He gave the man her address, then took something out of his pocket. It was a small gold locket. He flicked it open. "This is what she looks like."

The man glanced at the locket and examined the portrait inside.

"Very good, m'lord."

"I want to know if anyone is following her, and I want to know that she is safe. You will be working with Peggy Black as usual. It will be up to the two of you to watch over her."

"Yes, m'lord."

The man bowed himself out of the room.

Justin stood alone, thinking for a few minutes. As he did so, his eyes strayed to Cassandra's portrait and he looked at it for the thousandth time. The artist had caught her clear blue eyes and had added the tiny flecks of gold that made them so unusual, and he had caught her hair, making it soft and golden. He had painted her skin so well that as Justin stroked his finger over it he could almost feel the soft touch of it.

He remembered the first time he had seen the portrait. The locket had burst open when Rupert Paxton had thrown it down on to a gaming table to cover a bet. Rupert had had four kings. Justin had had four aces. He had won the locket fair and square. Even so, he had not meant to keep it. For a day or two, yes, to teach Rupert a lesson, but then he had meant to return it: he was not in the habit of keeping personal possessions won from young fools at the gambling tables. But somehow he had not been able to part with it.

CHAPTER FIVE

Despite her misgivings about Maria's tendency to matchmake, Cassandra found herself looking forward to the soirée. It would be one of her last few chances to enjoy herself and she meant to make the most of it. She also had to admit to herself that she was looking forward to seeing Lord Deverill.

She looked through her gowns, trying to decide which one would be the most appropriate for the evening. The white muslin she had already worn, which left the blue spotted muslin or the jonquil satin. Knowing how much Maria disliked the jonquil, she decided on the blue spot. It was a little short, but it was otherwise unexceptionable. Its short, puffed sleeves were edged with lace, and there was a matching row of lace decorating the high waistline. With a scoop neckline and a long, narrow skirt, it was fashionable enough, and with her blue satin shoes it would make a pass-able outfit.

She slipped her chemise over her head then put on her drawers and corset, standing still whilst Moll laced it up. Then she put up her arms as Moll slipped the gown over her head, and dropped them as Moll fastened the buttons at the back. She sat in front of the dressing table so that Moll could thread a blue ribbon through her golden chignon, and then pulled on her gloves.

"You're ready early," said Moll, as Cassandra glanced at the clock.

"Maria asked me to arrive in good time. Her housekeeper hasn't been well, and I promised I would help with any last minute arrangements."

Moll nodded approvingly.

Cassandra picked up her fan and went downstairs, to find John waiting in the hall. He was a stocky man in late middle age, and had been with the family for as long as Cassandra could remember. He had put her on her first horse, and had refused to leave her when her parents died. "You need a man about the house," he'd said, when Rupert had left for Brighton, and he had stayed.

"Has the coach been properly mended?" she asked him, as the two of them went outside.

"Yes, miss They've done a good job of it. That wheel won't come off again in a hurry."

"Good."

John opened the door and let down the step, and Cassandra climbed inside. The coach was a ponderous equippage, not like Maria's smart new carriage, but it was serviceable, and they were soon on their way.

Maria's house was in one of the less fashionable parts of town, but it was very smart inside. A narrow hall with a straight staircase led upstairs, and Cassandra was taken up by a liveried footman. Once upstairs the rooms were of a good size, and were elegantly proportioned. Gold paper covered the walls in the drawing-room, an oriental rug covered the polished floorboards, and lacquered furniture completed the oriental theme.

"It's the Prince who revived the craze for chinoiserie," said Maria, as she greeted Cassandra. "Harry loves it, so we have installed it throughout the house."

"I like it," said Cassandra approvingly. "It's very different from the gilded furniture you had the last time I was here. And the conservatory is lovely," she said, looking through the door and noticing the new addition to the house, which had been built over the kitchen.

"Isn't it? You must let me show it to you."

Maria led the way proudly into the conservatory, her silk gown rustling as she walked. Her gown was a wonderful creation in a shade of deep rose, and it was decorated with artificial flowers and foliage. Over it, she wore a shawl embroidered with silver, and to complement it, she wore a few simple flowers tucked into her hair.

"I suppose I ought to wear a turban," she remarked, as Cassandra said how well she looked, "but I can never quite get used to them. Besides, Harry doesn't like them. He says they make me look old."

"Where is Harry?" asked Cassandra.

"He is seeing to the wine. He is terrified Hingis will serve his best claret and is overseeing him as he brings the bottles up from the cellar."

They passed into the conservatory. Although small, it had a selection of exotic plants and a few choice pieces of furniture, tastefully arranged.

"I must remember to replace the candles," said Maria, glancing at the wax candles which had burnt down to stubs. "I have so many things to remember! It's such a relief that you've come early. I've had to spend the afternoon organizing the servants, and even so, some things have been left undone."

"What do you need me to do?" asked Cassandra, after exclaiming over the conservatory.

"If you could see to the candles—no, wait, the cards need putting out first. I've set up a card room for the gentlemen," she explained. "Can you set out new packs of cards for me?"

"Of course," said Cassandra.

"Good. Then I can make sure that Cook is almost ready."

Cassandra went into the card-room as Maria departed to speak to her cook. The card-room had been set up in a small ante-room opening off the drawing-room, and four card-tables had been set up in its centre. A candelabra on each ensured good light, but as yet the cards had not been put out. Cassandra looked round. There was no sign of them. She went over to a beaureau at the side of the room and, opening a drawer, found what she was looking for. She set out the crisp new cards, one pack on each table. Then she went through into the drawing-room again. One of the footmen was there. Instructing him to replace the candles in the conservatory, she then set about organizing two further footmen as they arranged the room ready for the concert. A small dais had already been erected at one end, and Cassandra made sure the chairs were placed in rows in front of it. She arranged the music stand and then stood back to view the effect.

"Oh, yes, that's just right," said Maria, hurrying in, just as the long-case clock in the hall struck the hour. "Thank you, Cassie. I thought I would never be done. Now, Madame Lorette should be here with her harp in a few minutes. It will give her time to tune her instrument before the guests arrive."

Sure enough, there was a commotion downstairs, and a few minutes later Madame Lorette swept into the room. She was an imposing woman with a heaving bosom, who was resplendent in scarlet. Her gown was ruched at the sides to reveal a white underskirt, and was matched by a scarlet turban adorned with a white feather. After much difficulty, her harp was manouevred upstairs, and she began to tune her instrument. As the rippling notes filled the room, Cassandra was pleased to see that Maria relaxed.

"Now everything is ready," said Maria. "Our first guests can arrive."

It was a small, select gathering. Cassandra recognized a number of young ladies from her seminary and was soon busy talking to them about their favourite mistresses, whilst sharing fond reminiscences of the dancing master.

"A lucky man," came a soft voice behind her, and Cassandra saw that Lord Deverill had joined her. "He had the opportunity of dancing with you before I did."

"I don't think he was really so fortunate," said Cassandra with a smile. "I found it almost impossible to learn the cotillion, and I kept stepping on his toes!"

Lord Deverill laughed.

"Do you enjoy music?" she asked him, as she saw him glance towards Madame Lorette.

"Very much. I used to have a box at the opera. Have you ever been?"

"Yes, I went with my family."

She found the conversation flowed easily. They talked of the museums and galleries, the theatres and parks, all the things Cassandra had seen on her one visit to the capital. Lord Deverill was knowledgeable and interesting.

At length they took their seats for the concert. Maria introduced Madame Lorette, there was a smattering of applause, and then the conversation died away as Madame Lorette began.

Lord Deverill turned his attention to the music. Cassandra, too, was enjoying the concert, but all the time she was aware of Lord Deverill sitting next to her. She didn't know how it was, but he affected her in ways no man had ever done before. She seemed to have an awareness of him that was entirely new to her. It was alarming and pleasurable at the same time. She turned to look at him. His face, seen in profile, was strong, but around the eyes something softer lurked.

The recital came to an end and there was enthusiastic applause. Cassandra was about to comment on the music when Lord Deverill was accosted by a dowager, who expressed herself volubly on the subject of harps. Seeing Maria close by, Cassandra went over to her friend and complimented her on the evening.

"I am so relieved that everything is going well," said Maria. "Madame Lorette played admirably. But that is not the best thing. The best thing is that Lord Deverill is clearly enchanted with you. And he is not the only one. I distinctly saw Lord Armington looking in your direction when he arrived, and he has asked if he can take you into supper. Two earls, Cassie! You are one of the most popular young ladies in Brighton."

Lord Armington walked over to join them. He was immaculately dressed in satin breeches and a satin tailcoat.

"Might I have the honour of taking you in to supper?" he asked, bowing over Cassandra's hand.

Cassandra saw Maria mouthing the words, "Try, Cassie," behind his back.

Cassandra gave an inward sigh, but knowing it would be rude to refuse, she accepted Lord Armington's invitation.

Maria's cook had excelled herself, and there were many flattering comments on the food. After everyone had eaten their fill, the party began to split up into groups. Some people went into the card-room to play whilst others indulged in conversations.

Soon the guests would wander into the conservatory, thought Cassandra. Wanting to make sure the footman had replaced the candles as she had instructed, she excused herself.

"I must help Maria," she said to Lord Armington.

He bowed politely, and she went into the conservatory. She was pleased to see that her orders had been carried out. The candles were new, and had just been lit. They cast a warm glow over the exotic green foliage and the carefully placed furniture. She was about to return to the drawing-room when she found that she was not alone. One of the younger gentlemen had followed her, and was propping himself up against a tall urn.

"Miss Paxton," he said in a slurred voice.

"Mr. Bradley."

Mr. Bradley was the son of a wealthy manufacturer, and heir to a vast fortune. His clothes were exquisite, but reflected the most outlandish taste. His tailcoat was adorned with huge gilt buttons and his shoes were capped with rosettes. His stockings were gold, and his waistcoat was dazzling. But despite this magnificence, she eyed him warily. He was clearly drunk, and young gentlemen in their cups could prove difficult to manage.

"I was just about to join the company," she said.

He took a tottering step into the room.

"No need to do that just yet," he said. "Come to talk to you about—hic!—selling your town house."

"Ah." Here was a piece of good fortune. "I'm glad to know you're interested in it. It's a fine house, close to the sea. It's been very well cared for, and is furnished with style. My brother had excellent taste."

"I might be interested in buying it," he said, lurching towards her.

She smelt the alcohol on his breath.

"You must see my lawyer—"

"Come now, no need for lawyers. Thought we could fix it up between the two of us. Just you and me. Thought I could come round and see it. I could come tonight," he said tapping his nose with his finger, or at least attempting to, for he was too drunk to accomplish the feat. "No one the wiser. Come when the servants are in bed. See the whole place. See the drawing-room. See the bedroom," he leered.

"Mr. Bradley, you're drunk," she said with a sigh.

"Not too drunk to know a pretty girl when I see one," he said, making a lunge for her. He snaked his arm round her waist and pressed his face close to hers. She turned away in disgust, unwrapping his arm as she did so.

"No need to be like that. No shame in needing money. Well, I've—hic!—got it. You can name your price."

"The house will be offered—"

"I'm not talking about the house. I'm talking about the house with you inside it."

"I don't understand you," she said, drawing herself up and hoping her cold tone would return him to his senses.

"Oh, you understand me all right. I'll set you up there as my . . . my mistress," he said, swaying precariously. "You can have anything you want." He waved his arms. "Anything. Pair of matched bays. Four matched bays. Six matched bays," he said expansively, almost toppling over. "A carriage. Fine clothes. All the clothes you want."

"Mr. Bradley, I'm going back to the drawing-room now," she said firmly.

"What about a little kiss?" he said, leaning towards her.

"Absolutely not," she said.

His face became belligerent, and for the first time in the encounter she began to feel uneasy. His ridiculousness was fast wearing off, to be replaced by something uglier. She was not ignorant of drunkards and their moods and she could sense something menacing behind Mr. Bradley's manner. She edged round him, hoping to get past him and go through into the drawing-room, for she felt it was time to bring the episode to a speedy end. But he moved surprisingly quickly and he cut her off.

"Just a li'le kiss," he said.

Cassandra edged over to a pot which was displayed on a console table and contained a small palm. It would be very useful for crashing down on Mr. Bradley's head. But before she could reach it he flung his arms round her and they closed round her with surprising strength. He thrust his face into her own and fastened his lips on hers. She turned her head and fought him off. Breaking free, she ran to the door, but he reached it before her and slammed it shut. His face broke into a leer. He rubbed his hands together.

"A bit of a—hic!—game."

Unable to get past him she made for the pot, grasping it firmly in both hands and lifting it over her head. She was just wondering whether she should go towards Mr. Bradley menacingly or hope her actions would warn him to stay away when the door opened, knocking Mr. Bradley off balance, and glancing towards it she saw Lord Deverill.

"What the devil's going on here?" he asked, lifting one eyebrow. But beneath his light tone there was a note of steel.

"Mind your own damn business," said Mr. Bradley. "Miss Paxton and I were just having a bit of fun. You're not welcome here, Deverill."

"A pity," he drawled, "because I've a mind to stay."

Mr. Bradley lunged at him but he stepped aside and then, seizing a vase of flowers, he removed the flowers and flung the water in Mr. Bradley's face.

Mr. Bradley started backwards, rubbing the water out of his eyes.

"You bloody—"

He started to advance on Lord Deverill, who raised one eyebrow. Mr. Bradley hesitated.

"I think you owe Miss Paxton an apology," said Lord Deverill.

"What for?" asked Mr. Bradley belligerently.

"For insulting her."

"Never did anything of the kind," muttered Mr. Bradley sulkily.

"No?" asked Lord Deverill with a smile that bordered on the dangerous. "Unfortunately, I don't share your opinion. You will apologize to the lady."

Mr. Bradley looked up at Lord Deverill's implacable face and his bravado left him.

"I apologize," he muttered.

"Apology accepted," said Cassandra.

She put down the pot, returning it to its original position.

"Now I suggest you go back to your father. And one last thing, Bradley. You've had enough wine for one day."

Mr. Bradley looked sulky, then slunk out of the room.

"Are you all right?" asked Lord Deverill, going over to her.

"Yes. Thankfully you came in just in time. I was prepared to hit him over the head with the pot"—she smiled suddenly—"but I'm glad I didn't have to break one of Maria's prized possessions!"

He laughed.

"With luck, it would have broken Bradley's head first!"

Cassandra laughed, too. Then her laughter died away and there was an awkward silence. He was standing very close to her, and it made her feel on edge. Whether it was the fear left over from Mr. Bradley's behaviour or the energy left over from preparing to defend herself she did not know, but she somehow found that her pulse was racing and her breathing was shallow.

"When you offered me your help the other day, I did not know I would need it so soon," she said.

"No. Neither did I. Bradley's a fool with more money than sense, but he's nothing worse than that. Take no notice of him."

"No, I think it is better not to."

She was aware of his gaze resting on her; indeed he seemed to be finding difficulty taking his eyes away from her. She tried to meet his gaze, but she was suddenly abashed. Dropping her eyes, she traced the pattern of the rug on the floor.

"I hope it hasn't spoilt your enjoyment of the evening?" he said at last.

There was a rough edge to his voice, and she felt it sending a shiver down her spine.

"No," she said, and to her surprise, her voice came out with a quaver.

"Good. There are some foolish young men in Brighton, but they are not worth noticing."

He was standing so close to her that she could feel the heat of him and she put her hand to her hair, instinctively playing with a strand that had fallen loose to calm her rapidly beating pulse. He raised his hand, too, and their fingers touched. She dropped her hand as though scalded, but his continued to rise and tangled itself in her golden tresses.

For Cassandra, the world stopped. She could see him and only him, highlighted in her suddenly narrowed vision, and she could feel nothing but the soft touch of his fingers. She ought to tell him to stop; she ought to pull away; but she could not do it. She couldn't even breathe, let alone move. She could only watch his face, mesmerized, as she took in the slight changes in his expression. She saw the curve of his mouth as it opened slightly, noticed the whiteness of his teeth and the fullness of his lips, and took in the slight shadow around his chin. She had never been so close to a man before. When dancing, she stood the required distance from her partner, and when talking she had always been separated by the space of a few feet of air. But here, there was so little distance between them that when he took a small step nearer she could feel the fabric of his coat brushing against the front of her dress. She felt the soft touch of his breath on her forehead as she tilted her face upwards, feeling it feather its way down to her cheeks and then to her lips. Instinctively they began to part. She felt his fingers stilling, and then to her painful disappointment she sensed, rather than saw, him stepping backwards. She felt empty, as though something vital had been taken from her just as it was about to be given.

She made an effort to master herself and opened her eyes. He was still very close to her, so that she could see him with great clarity, and she noticed he was holding something. It was a small piece of foliage.

She gave an inward sigh, as she realized that was why he had stepped so close. Making an effort to recover her composure she wondered why she had been so foolish, allowing herself to become mesmerized by a man who had done nothing more than remove a leaf from her hair.

"It must have fallen from the pot when I held it over my head," she said.

"Yes," he said.

But somehow the tension did not relax. He was still looking at her intently and she swallowed.

"Cassandra . . ." he said.

"Lord Deverill . . ."

"My name is Justin," he said softly.

"Justin . . . I . . ."

But she said no more, for without her knowing quite how it happened he was kissing her on the lips and she found herself responding, moving her mouth under his. It was a sweet sensation, slow and sensuous, and she slid her arms around his neck, revelling in the feeling until he let her go.

She looked into his eyes and saw the dark rim she had never been close enough to notice before, accentuating the green and making it glow. But she saw something else, a tortured look she could not understand, unless it was caused by the fact that he had kissed her and should not have done so.

The thought brought her to an awareness of what had happened and she felt herself flush. She had forgotten how to behave. For one mad moment she had lost control of herself and given in to her desires, desires she had never experienced before. They had overwhelmed her, intoxicating her and awakening her to new and powerful feelings.

It had all seemed so clear at the time: Justin was kissing her and she was kissing him back. But in the cold light of reality it seemed confusing, and she could take no more.

"I must go," she said.

She slipped out of the room, and returned to the drawing-room. It was noisy, so she retreated to the card-room, where there were only a few people. Some were playing cribbage and some whist. She stood and watched the players, effacing herself in the corner so that she would not be called upon to speak to anyone. By and by the ordinariness of her surroundings began to calm her and she felt her pulse slow. She began to take an interest in the games, and was pleased to see a game of cribbage brought to a successful conclusion.

She had just restored her equanimity, however, when it was shaken again by the sight of Mr. Bradley entering the room. He was looking a trifle more sober than the last time she had seen him. He had fastened the buttons of his waistcoat and straightened his cravat. But she was still wary of him. He looked round the room, and his eyes alighted on her. In the card-room, with others present, she did not feel threatened, but she was uncomfortable nonetheless, particularly when he came and stood next to her. Like her, he watched the games. Or at least pretended to.

"You think Deverill's such a hero," he said, "but you don't know the first thing about him, and you wouldn't like it if you knew. I'm not the only young man he's threatened. He does it all the time. He's a bully."

Cassandra bit back an angry retort, fearing it would only make him worse.

He sneered. "You don't believe me," he said. "I can see it in your eyes. You think I'm making it up, but I can soon prove it to you." He never took his eyes off the game, but spoke to her in a low undertone. "Ask Deverill where he was last year, on the night your brother died."

"I know where he was. He was with Rupert."

He looked surprised. "So you know about that. I'm surprised he told you. I didn't think he would. I thought he'd keep something like that to himself. But if that's the case, I don't know how you can bear to let him look at you. There's no need to play the innocent," he jeered, turning towards her. "You know what I mean. He can't keep his eyes off you. He can't keep his hands off you, either, I'll be bound. You were a long time in the conservatory once I'd left. What were you doing in there?" He glanced at the low neck of her gown. "That lace around your neck wasn't crooked before."

Cassandra was tempted to strike him, but kept her hands by her side.

"It's lucky no one else noticed," he said, "or what would it do to your reputation? Not as unsoiled as you like to appear, are you?"

"You have said enough," said Cassandra, moving away from him.

"Ask Deverill what he was doing with your brother on the night he died. Ask him what really happened, then see how much you want him to touch you."

"What do you mean? And how do you know Lord Deverill was with Rupert the night he died?"

"Because Raistrick talks when he's in his cups."

"Mr. Raistrick said nothing about it to me."

"Perhaps you didn't ask?"

Mr. Bradley moved away, but the damage had been done. What did he mean? What more did he know about Lord Deverill and her brother? Why should she not want him to touch her if she knew? Despite the fact that she didn't want to take any notice of Mr. Bradley's words she found she could not ignore them. Moreover, she found herself wondering if they had had anything to do with the tortured look in Justin's eyes.

~ ~ ~

Justin remained in the conservatory long after Cassandra was gone, feeling low in spirits. He should not have given in to his feelings and kissed her. It was not the way he should have behaved towards a gently reared young lady. But when he had seen her in danger it had aroused his protective instincts, and when he had seen that she was shaken he had wanted to soothe her. He had not meant to touch her, but when he had seen the leaf in her hair he had removed it without thinking about what he was doing. As he had felt the softness of her tresses, other instincts had been aroused, and before he had had time to think about it he had taken her into his arms and kissed her.

He had had no right to do it. He was not betrothed to her, nor could he ever become betrothed to her.

Leaving the conservatory, he glimpsed Cassandra through the door of the card-room. In the candlelight her hair was glowing with golden lights. Her skin was soft and smooth, and he longed to kiss her again, but he must never do so. He must fight his attraction, because it was an unwanted complication in an already tangled situation.

He turned away from the sight and went to find Maria.

"Mrs. Winter, this has been a splendid soirée. Thank you for inviting me," he said politely.

"You're surely not going so soon?" asked Maria.

"Alas, I have some business to attend to."

"Oh, what a pity. Never mind, I'm delighted you could come. I'm sure Miss Paxton is delighted, too. I hope you will honour one of our little gatherings again?"

"I would be delighted," he said.

Then, having done his duty, he departed, leaving Cassandra—but not his turbulent feelings—behind him.

~ ~ ~

Cassandra went into the drawing-room, feeling shaken by what she had heard. As she did so, she noticed that a number of guests were floating towards the stairs. The party was breaking up, and carriages were being called. She looked round, but could not see Justin. With a sinking feeling she realized that he had already gone.

Maria and Harry were bidding their guests farewell.

"Thank you for a marvellous evening," said a woman who was resplendent in a gold silk gown.

"I'm so glad you enjoyed it," said Maria. "Do come again."

Harry added his endorsement, and sped the guests on their way.

"What a wonderful harpist you found for us, Maria. I must hire her myself," said an officer in uniform.

"Yes, isn't she good?" said Maria. "I will give you her direction."

"A fine supper, Maria. You must let my cook have the recipe for your salmon tart."

"I'll ask her to send it round tomorrow."

The guests departed, and at last the house was empty. Chairs had been pushed aside and were scattered haphazardly across the floor. The music stand had fallen over, and empty glasses were piled on a tray by the door. A harassed footman picked up the tray and carried it out of the room.

"What a relief!" said Maria, collapsing on to a chaise longue. "I enjoyed myself immensely, but I am exhausted."

"It all went very well, I thought," said Harry.

"Yes, it was excellent," said Cassandra. "I heard a number of people saying how much they'd enjoyed themselves."

"I'm so pleased. It's always a worry, and when Mrs. Gunning fell ill I thought I would never manage. But it all went very well. Madame Lorette played superbly, I thought."

"She did. And the supper was excellent," said Cassandra.

Maria gave a happy sigh.

"Even so, I am glad we are not entertaining again for a while," she said. "It will take me at least a week to get over it. Lord Armington was attentive, I thought," she added, turning to Cassandra.

Cassandra had forgotten about Lord Armington. So much had happened since she sat next to him during supper that it seemed almost a week ago.

"Yes, he was," she conceded, adding, "just as he was attentive to every other lady in the room."

"Even so, I have high hopes," said Maria. "He remarked on your beauty to Harry, and he told me that it is time for him to take a wife. If that is not meaningful, then I don't know what is." She paused. "Lord Deverill was also very attentive. I didn't see anything of him after supper until he took his leave of me. But these great men do as they please. To think, I had two lords in my drawing-room, and both at the same time!"

Cassandra said nothing about Justin's activities after supper. She had no intention of revealing what had happened between them. To many young ladies, attracting the attentions of an earl would be a source of unalloyed happiness, but Cassandra found it unsettling. A gentleman who talked to her about books and poetry as Lord Armington did was one thing; a gentleman who made her tremble with his touch was quite another.

She thought back to his kiss. It had been unsettling and disturbing and wonderful. And then she remembered the moment he had pulled away from her, and remembered the expression in his eyes. It was almost as though he had kissed her against his will, and as though he had regretted it.

She had been kissed twice that evening, but both times had been completely different. Mr. Bradley had wanted to impose his will on hers, to take something she had no desire to give. He had wanted her in his power. But there had been nothing of power in Justin's kiss, only a tender yearning and a smouldering fire.

Mr. Bradley's perplexing words intruded on her thoughts. She knew that Mr. Bradley had been trying to unsettle her, but even so, when he had spoken to her in the card-room there had been something in his eye that had told her he was not just making mischief. There was something behind his words.

She shivered.

"Cold?" asked Maria.

"A little," she said.

"I'm not surprised. It's late."

Maria yawned.

"I should be going," said Cassandra. "You must want the house to yourselves."

"Not at all," said Maria. "You are welcome to stay the night."

"No, thank you, it's time for me to leave."

"I will call the carriage," said Maria.

Cassandra put on her shawl and took her leave of Maria and Harry, but as she left the house she felt her spirits sink. It was clear that Justin regretted kissing her. As she went home, she wondered if she would ever see him again.

CHAPTER SIX

The same thoughts were troubling her the following morning. She had slept badly and awoken unrefreshed, so that she was only too glad to get up and start the day. Going downstairs, she went into the parlour. To her pleasure, she found something to break her low mood, because there, propped up on the breakfast table, was a letter. She recognized the scrawling handwriting at once. It was from her sister, Lizzie.

She picked it up and carried it over to the window to read. A shaft of sunlight fell on the uneven letters, which trailed across the paper like a drunken spider. Each page was crossed and difficult to make out, but Cassandra at last managed to decipher it.

"I've brung you chocolate and rolls," said Moll, carrying a tray into the room.

"Thank you, Moll."

"You've seen it, then?" she asked, setting the tray down on the table.

"Yes," said Cassandra, scanning the closely written pages.

"Is she enjoying herself?" asked Moll.

"Yes, very much. Sit down, I'll read it to you," said Cassandra, taking her place at the table.

With a familiarity that would have appalled most employers, Moll did as Cassandra bid her. She proceeded to take a plate of hot rolls and a cup of chocolate from the tray and set them down in front of Cassandra, then wiped her hands on her apron and listened with rapt attention as Cassandra began to read.

Darling, darling, Cassie.

"Ah." Moll nodded approvingly.

Cassandra took a sip of chocolate and then continued to read.

I am having a WUNDERFUL time. Jane has lent me her pony and he is far better than old fat Tom, thow I love old Tom dearly. He is called Prince. Are you married yet? Jane says everywun gets a husband in Brighton even if they are old and rinkly and you are not so you will find a husband I am

shaw. I sed to Jane you don't want one but she says everywun
wants a husband and I wish you wud get married as long as
you don't marry HORRID HORRID HORRID Mr. Brown.

Cassie almost spilled her chocolate. She knew she should
be appalled by her sister's atrocious spelling, but she was
instead amused by Lizzie's lively letter.

HORRID HORRID HORRID Mr. Brown was their nearest country neighbour, and he had taken to haunting their
house since Rupert had died. Using the library as an excuse
for his visits, he had borrowed and returned books until
Cassandra and Lizzie were heartily sick of him, leading
Lizzie to remark crossly that he always had his nose stuck in
a book.

He had then astonished Cassandra by offering her marriage. The fact that he was fifty years old had not stopped
him as, he had kindly informed her, he did not consider
their relative ages a problem. Indeed, he had told Cassandra
that he could overlook her youth and inexperience in view
of the fact he was sure she would soon settle down into a useful housewife. He had been surprised when she had refused
him; so surprised, in fact, that he had asked her twice more,
just to be sure. And if she had not left home, she feared he
would have asked her twice more again.

"I don't say she's right for calling him horrid," said Moll,
with the air of one determined to be just, "but he's an old

man and a regular nuisance, there's no gainsaying. Now finish your breakfast before you say another word."

Forbearing to point out that she was two and twenty, and that she had left the nursery well and truly behind her, Cassandra meekly finished her breakfast. Then she continued to read Lizzie's letter. Moll nodded sagely at everything that could be construed as a compliment towards the little girl, whether it be the fact that Jane's papa had called her a taking little thing, or the fact that Jane's sister—a haughty young lady of thirteen years old—had said that she was very stupid, but not as stupid as Jane.

When the letter was finished, nothing would do for Moll but that Cassandra should read it again.

The clock chimed the hour.

"I must get on," said Cassandra. She looked out of the window. "It's a beautiful morning. I think I'll go to the circulating library before making a start on the drawing-room."

"I'll fetch my bonnet," said Moll.

Ten minutes later the two of them set out. There were a number of circulating libraries in Brighton. The oldest of them was on the east side of the Steyne. Books could be bought or borrowed there and Cassandra had often visited it with her family in happier times, for there was a billiard-room attached to it which had occupied Rupert and her father whilst she and her mother had chosen their books. On occasions she and her mother had been known to play a game of billiards as well. But it was not to this library that she was now going, for she was going to the newer library on the south side of the Steyne. There were a number of excellent shops in the vicinity and, whilst purchasing anything was out of the question, Cassandra was looking forward to admiring the displays in the windows.

The morning was cool and the fashionable visitors who were promenading along the Steyne were wrapped up in colourful spencers. They looked pointedly at a group of men who were playing cricket, as if to say, "Go and play your games elsewhere." It was an old problem. Rupert had often played cricket on the Steyne and had frequently fallen foul of promenaders who took exception to dodging cricket balls, or being knocked down by enthusiastic fielders.

Cassandra was just about to cross the open space when she saw Justin walking towards her with his hound trotting by his side. He checked on seeing her, and she felt herself torn in two. After their encounter in the conservatory any meeting between them would necessarily be difficult, and with Mr. Bradley's words haunting her it was even more disturbing, but she could not help feeling glad to see him again.

He tipped his hat.

"Miss Paxton, he said.

"Lord Deverill," she acknowledged him.

She stood awkwardly, searching for a neutral topic of conversation to try and convince him that she was at ease. And then, to her relief, the hound nudged her hand with his wet nose and demanded her attention.

"He's a fine animal," she said, as she stroked him behind the ears.

"He is," he said. "He belongs to my sister."

"Oh! I thought he was yours."

"Alas, no. The town house isn't big enough for me to keep a hound, but I look after Troilus whenever my sister is away. She lives nearby, on her husband's estate, but she is in London at the moment."

"It seems like a useful arrangement."

"It is. It suits us both. I have the benefit of Troilus's company, and my sister is relieved of the worry that the servants will overfeed him."

"And do they overfeed him?" asked Cassandra, looking at his sleek figure.

"No, but Anne is convinced that everyone indulges him when her back is turned. The irony is that she cannot resist giving him titbits herself," he said with a ghost of a smile.

Cassandra appreciated his attempt to lighten the situation, and said, "He looks well on it."

"Yes, he does. Are you going far?" he asked, introducing a new subject as the old one showed signs of fading away.

"To the library," she said.

She was beginning to feel a little more comfortable. Even so, memories of Mr. Bradley's words prevented her from being truly at ease. She reminded herself that she knew very little about Justin. She knew that she was drawn to him but she did not want the attraction to cloud her judgement. She would have liked to ask him about Mr. Bradley's comments but out in public, and with Moll so close, it was impossible to raise the subject, and she knew she would have to wait for a more private time.

"Are you looking for any books in particular?" he asked.

"I must confess that I'm hoping to find something by Mrs. Radcliffe."

"*The Mysteries of Udolpho*, perhaps?"

"No, I've already read that."

"And did you enjoy it?"

"Yes. It sent shivers down my spine. I loved the sword fight."

"And the catacombs?"

"You've read it?" she asked.

"My sister devours everything Mrs. Radcliffe writes. I was so tired of hearing her talk about books I knew nothing about, I decided I must read them as well."

"You mean you didn't lock them up and forbid her to touch them?"

"No. Nor did I lock *her* up and forbid her to touch them!"

"Then you have sadly missed your opportunity," she said. "You could have figured as The Evil Guardian."

"Modelled after Count Montoni, perhaps?" he asked, raising one eyebrow.

"I do see a certain resemblance," said Cassandra.

She did not know how it was, but their natural rapport seemed to have overcome their awkwardness to such an extent that she had felt able to make a joke. But now she wished it unsaid. She had gone too far. But one look at his face showed her that he did not mind.

"I will have to tell my sister. She will be most amused . . . and glad to find someone so like-minded," he said.

She smiled.

"If she really thought you like the wicked count, I don't think she would have entrusted her hound to you."

"No. *Now*, she likes me very well. But when I wouldn't let her run away with her dancing master at the tender age of fifteen, she thought me an ogre, I can assure you!"

"She will not thank you for telling me that."

"Then I must hope you never mention it to her," he said.

"I promise I won't."

Cassandra reminded herself that she should not be talking to him in this easy manner, and said, "I must not detain you."

"Nor I you."

He made her a bow and bade her farewell, then walked on.

"A nice spoken gennulmen," said Moll, looking after him.

"Don't tell me you approve of him?" said Cassandra.

"There's them that are worse," said Moll gruffly.

"I'm sure he would be delighted to hear it."

"Seems to bump into us regular," said Moll.

"And what's that supposed to mean?"

"Nothing," said Moll.

Cassandra looked at her suspiciously, but Moll assumed an innocent expression.

Cassandra resumed her walk to the library. When she reached the building a group of young ladies were coming out, talking and giggling. They were followed by a harassed-looking footman who could barely see where he was going for the enormous pile of books he was carrying. When they had let the group pass, Cassandra and Moll went into the library. Moll took a seat at the side of the room, not being interested in novels, and Cassandra was free to wander round by herself.

As she looked at the books, she thought that she had valued her conversation with Justin far more than any of the conversations she had had with Lord Armington and Mr. Kingsley. And yet there was a dark side to him, too, and she knew she would do well to remember it.

She chose her books, and half an hour later she emerged with a selection of them under her arm. Moll followed behind, carrying another two.

"Although when I'll find time to read them, I don't know," said Cassandra regretfully. "I must beat the carpets this afternoon. I will get nothing done tomorrow."

"A good thing you and Miss Maria are going to the races," said Moll. "You shouldn't be doing all this work, Miss Cassie."

"Never mind, it will soon be finished," she said, as they walked along by the sea.

"And a good thing, too," said Moll.

But Cassandra did not think it a good thing, because once it was finished she would have no excuse to stay in Brighton. She would have to instruct her lawyer to see to the sale, and then she must return to her estate.

~ ~ ~

"I've laid the sprig muslin out on the bed for you," said Moll the following morning, as Cassandra emerged from her dressing room, newly washed and dressed in her chemise. "Though mind you wear a shawl. That muslin's as thin as a cobweb, and you'll catch your death otherwise, just see if you don't."

"I'll be sure to wear it," Cassandra promised her.

The day was warm but she intended to follow Moll's advice, not because she feared pneumonia, but because there was a scorch mark on the back of the dress. It had been caused by an unfortunate accident with the flat iron, and she needed a shawl to cover it. She slipped into her muslin and Moll fastened it. Then, settling a straw hat on her head, Cassandra tied it beneath her chin with a wide green ribbon. No sooner had she fastened it in place than she heard a sound of a carriage. Maria had arrived. She pulled on her gloves.

"Don't forget your parasol," said Moll.

Cassandra took it from her, then tripped outside.

The weather had favoured her since the start of her stay, and the sun was bright and strong. A gentle breeze blew from the sea, fluttering the ends of her ribbons.

"Do you know Geoffrey Goddard?" she asked Harry conversationally as she climbed into the carriage and they set out for Whitehawk Down.

"No, I don't think I do. Why?" Harry asked.

"I believe he'll be at the races today. He knew Rupert," she explained.

"You mustn't dwell on the past," said Maria robustly to Cassandra. "Rupert is dead, and there's no reason why you should seek out Mr. Goddard . . . unless, of course, he is eligible," she mused.

"Maria," said Harry reprovingly.

"What's wrong?" asked Maria innocently. "I just want what's best for Cassie, that's all."

"Thank you, but I can decide on what's best for myself," said Cassandra, with a quirk at the corner of her mouth. "I don't want to marry Mr. Goddard. I just want to speak to him," she went on. "I won't be in Brighton for much longer, and I don't want to miss the opportunity of seeing him."

The carriage rolled through the streets. There had been a great deal of building work carried out since Cassandra's last visit, and fashionable houses were springing up here and there.

Cassandra's eyes ran over a new crescent. The houses were four storeys tall with elegant balconies ornamenting the first floor windows and smart black railings separating them from the street. Their bowed fronts broke up the monotony of line, and their windows gleamed in the sunlight. Chimneys were visible, rising from the rooftops, and they had an air of prosperity about them.

Gradually the carriage left the new houses behind and passed on to the old town. Here the brick and flint buildings were jostled together without any of the symmetry that marked the new houses, but they had a charm and character of their own. Then the carriage began to make its way up the winding road to Whitehawk Down.

The road was busy with Brighton's fashionable visitors, all travelling to the same destination, and it took them some time to reach it, but the view was worth waiting for. From the high vantage point, there was a splendid view of the sea.

The position had a disadvantage, however, for the wide open spaces of the Down allowed the wind easy access, and Cassandra had to put her hand on her head to stop her bonnet blowing off. She retied the green ribbon, making it tighter, then stepped out of the carriage.

There was already a great deal of activity on the Down, and numerous carriages were dotted about. Sporting curricles stood side by side with barouche landaus and high-perch phaetons. Their shafts rested on the ground, whilst the horses that had pulled them grazed quietly nearby. Ladies and gentlemen strolled around the course. The ladies' light dresses fluttered round their ankles, revealing an inch of embroidered stocking. Officers laughed noisily. Their scarlet and gold uniforms shone brightly in the sunshine.

A seedier set of people, in clothes that had once been good but now showed signs of wear, handed bundles of notes to sharp-looking men at the side of the course, whilst gaudily-painted women hung on their arms. A stand had been erected, and nearby, booths, stalls and tents had sprung up, offering every kind of food, drink and entertainment. Gin and ale competed with oysters and cakes for the money of the race-goers, and a hurdy gurdy man walked along, followed by a string of children.

"What a wretched noise!" said Maria, as she followed Cassandra out of the carriage. "I cannot abide it! I only hope he stops playing when the races begin."

Cassandra rather liked the raucous sound. It was so different to anything she experienced at home that she enjoyed the novelty, and it gave the outing a holiday atmosphere.

"I can't see the Prince," said Maria, looking about her. "What a pity. I hoped he might be here. He is very fond of the races. But never mind. Ah, here is someone interesting. It's Freddy Kingsley."

Mr. Kingsley was again dressed in the extreme of fashion. His gaudily coloured waistcoat showed beneath his coat of grey superfine, which was so tight it was a wonder he could move his arms. A tall hat was placed on his curled hair, and a silver-tipped cane was in his hand. His knee breeches gave way to silk stockings, and beneath them were black pumps.

"Dashed piece of luck, seeing you here," said Freddy, bowing over Cassandra's hand. "Been hoping to bump into you sometime or other ever since we danced together at the assembly. Enjoyed it immensely." He raised his quizzing glass and examined Cassandra's hat. "Dashed fine hat," he said. "Brim wide but not too wide. Ribbon at a jaunty angle. Sets the whole thing off." He greeted Maria and Harry politely, then said, "Care for a stroll?"

Cassandra accepted his arm, and Harry offered his arm to Maria, then the four of them took a stroll along the Downs. The delicious smells of fresh bread and pies mingled with the salty tang of the sea air.

"Get 'em while they're hot!" sang out the man behind the pie stall, a round individual who was a walking advertisement for his own wares.

A group of officers was standing and talking by the stall, with brightly painted women on their arms. One of the officers was holding a coin aloft.

"Look at that. It saved my life in France," he was saying. "I was trying to get home when the Peace broke down and a Frenchie took a shot at me. He would have got me, too, if not for the coin. I had it in my pocket and it stopped the bullet. Mind you, it left an imprint on my–"

He stopped abruptly.

"Oooh," squealed one of the women, whilst a bolder one laughed and said, "Show us, darlin'."

"Fans! Ivory fans! The genuine article, all the way from China!" cried one of the many vendors who walked through the crowds with trays round their necks.

A young woman with a low-cut dress who was flirting with a group of fashionably dressed men, giggled, "Oh, look at all the fans! And mine's just broken."

A chorus of male voices offered to buy her another one, and she laughed with them, praising the choice of one whilst rejecting the offering of another.

"What are her parents thinking of?" said Maria under her breath."

"Don't suppose they're here," said Mr. Kingsley. "Left her to the care of friends, most likely. No end of mischief a girl can get up to in Brighton."

Cassandra could understand what he meant. The gin tents and ale stalls had tipsy gentlemen nearby, and there were so many officers that it could easily turn a girl's head if she was not properly chaperoned. It was all colourful and noisy and, to Cassandra, who had not left the quiet and boredom of the country for years, quite wonderful.

"Ballad sheets!" exclaimed Cassandra, as a hawker walked past with a tray round his neck. "I must buy the latest one. Lizzie loves singing."

"Lizzie?" asked Mr. Kingsley.

"My sister—"

"Oh, look. There are some prints, and by a stroke of good fortune they are exactly what I have been looking for," said Maria, turning Mr. Kingsley's attention to another hawker. "Will you give me your arm, Mr. Kingsley? Cassandra can join us when she has chosen her ballad."

"Oh, er . . ."

"Lizzie is my younger sister, and she lives with me," said Cassandra firmly. "She is ten years old, and since my parents and brother died, I am all she has."

Maria had advised her not to mention her sister until she was sure of a gentleman's affections, but Cassandra did not like the idea of deceiving anyone. Lizzie was an important part of her life and she felt that the sooner Mr. Kingsley knew about the little girl the better.

"Oh," said Mr. Kingsley amiably. "Must let me buy her a ballad as well, then. Can't have too many."

Maria cast Cassandra a satisfied look.

"Do you know a gentleman by the name of Mr. Goddard?" asked Cassandra, when they had made their choice.

"Geoffrey Goddard? Seen him somewhere about. Saw him with Deverill earlier."

"Lord Deverill?"

"Yes. Tall chap. Black hair. Coat by Weston. Dashed fine cut."

"Yes, I know Lord Deverill. That is, we've met."

Freddy raised his quizzing glass and looked round the crowd. People were starting to make their way towards the track, ready for the race to begin, but one or two lingered round the stalls.

"There's Deverill now. Got Goddard with him. Coming this way," said Freddy.

Cassandra followed his glance and saw Justin coming towards her with a young man by his side. The two made a strong contrast. Justin, tall, well dressed in breeches and tailcoat, walking with assurance, and Mr. Goddard, almost as tall but gangly, dressed in a striped coat, embroidered waistcoat and tight breeches, and walking with a mincing gait.

"Miss Paxton," said Justin, as he drew level with her.

"Lord Deverill. We meet again."

"So we do," he said blandly. "Allow me to introduce Mr. Goddard."

"Pleased to make your acquaintance," said Mr. Goddard. "I've been wanting to speak to you ever since I knew you were in Brighton. Rupert and I were good friends. I miss him now he's gone. We all do."

Justin turned to Freddy.

"Kingsley, I wonder if you could help me. I'd like your advice."

"My advice?" asked Freddy, startled.

"Yes. I'm having trouble with my cravats. My valet's a clumsy fellow and he can't tie them for me, so I have to tie them myself. I can manage a barrel knot, but I've a fancy for something more elaborate. I want to try a waterfall, and since your cravats are always exquisitely tied, I thought I'd ask you how you manage it."

Freddy went pink with pleasure. To be asked for help! And by such a man! Then his smile gave way to a serious expression.

"It isn't easy," he said. "Don't you want to start with something simpler? The waterfall's a dashed tricky thing to do."

"No, it's the waterfall or nothing."

Freddy nodded. He lifted his hands to his neck and began to describe the intricacies of the style as Lord Deverill paid him flattering attention. Mr. Goddard offered Cassandra his arm, and the transition was smoothly accomplished: Lord Deverill walked in front with Freddy, whilst Cassandra walked behind with Geoffrey Goddard. Maria and Harry brought up the rear.

As they walked, Cassandra had an opportunity to ask Mr. Goddard about Rupert, and discover that he, too, thought Rupert's letter was nothing that need concern her.

"Been gambling too freely," he said with decision.

"I'm relieved," said Cassandra. "Although I hope it wasn't a bet that led him to his death."

"No, that was an accident. Terrible thing, but an accident," he said firmly. "Shouldn't have been riding at night . . . hard for ladies to understand . . . wanted to do it . . ."

"By which you mean it was a foolish fancy that cost him dear," she said with a sigh. "Poor Rupert." Her brow wrinkled. "But if he'd been gambling too freely, wouldn't I have found a large debt that had to be paid when he died?" It had not occurred to her before, but if her brother had taken his horse out in the dark because he had gambled on setting a new record for riding to London overnight, then he must have lost the bet. Yet she had found no evidence of a debt. "I don't want to have one come on me unexpectedly."

"Probably won the bet," said Mr. Goddard. "Bet a fortune on it raining in the morning. Went home. Realized it was a stupid thing to do. No way of knowing what the weather's going to do. Couldn't sleep. Drank a bottle or two. Wrote to you. Said he'd done something terrible. Expected to lose a deal of money. Then heard the rain. Spirits lifted. Screwed the paper up and stuffed it in his breeches pocket. Went outside to look at the rain. Pouring down. Won the bet. Forgot about the letter."

"Yes, I suppose it must have been something like that," said Cassandra.

It was now a year since her brother had written it, and as she could not find a trace of anything terrible having happened she supposed there must be nothing to it after all.

"Do you know why he went out riding at night?" she asked.

Mr. Goddard looked uneasy, then said, "Probably had an assignation."

She hesitated, then said, "Do you know why Lord Deverill was with him?"

"No," he said guilelessly. "Was Deverill with him? I didn't know."

Cassandra realized he would tell her nothing further, and small wonder: no gentleman would want to talk of such things to a lady. But at least now she knew that Rupert had done nothing truly terrible.

They reached the side of the track. Maria and Harry had overtaken them and were already there. Justin and Freddy were not far away. Justin had been joined by a pretty young lady with fair hair and dimples, dressed in a fetching bonnet lined with ruched silk, and a matching green silk gown. Next to the young lady was her complacent mama. It wasn't only Miss Kerrith who had set her cap at him, Cassandra realized.

As she thought it, she felt a stab of jealousy. She told herself not to be absurd. Justin had no feelings for her, and she had no right to have any feelings for him. But why then had he kissed her? asked a small voice inside.

She turned her attention away from him deliberately and bowed to several people she had met at the assembly. Then the horses began to gather.

"Fancy any of them?" asked Freddy, turning to Cassandra. "Grey's going well this season. Belongs to Lord Povington. Ridden by his groom. Favour it myself."

Cassandra interested herself in the horses, and remarked that she liked the looks of a neat black with a white star on its forehead.

"Put a wager on for you," said Mr. Kingsley. Wagers were being made up and down the race course. "Still think the bay will do it myself, but never contradict a lady."

He went over to a nearby booth and made a small wager for each of them, then returned to Cassandra's side. He did it with some difficulty, for the crowd was growing denser by the minute.

Cassandra cast her eye along the course. It was a demanding one, with a hairpin bend, and the race promised to be exciting.

The atmosphere changed as the horses took up their starting positions. Everyone in the crowd turned to look at the track, and a hush fell. Then the horses were off.

The bay quickly outstripped the other horses whilst her own horse was trapped in the middle of the group and Maria's horse trailed towards the rear. Then Maria's horse put on a spurt and overtook Cassandra's, the bay fell behind, and Cassandra's horse made up lost ground on the bend. Maria's horse fell behind again, the bay joined the leaders, and Cassandra's horse made a challenge for third position.

There was a thunder of hoofs as the horses raced towards them and the front runners went past. Cassandra's horse was amongst them. She turned her head to follow its progress . . . and then suddenly she was jostled from behind and was thrown forward into the path of the oncoming horses. Before she had time to react, she felt a firm hand on the back of her shawl, and she was pulled out of the way just in time. She looked round to see Justin behind her. Their eyes met, and she read something there that she could not understand. Then he took her hand and pulled her arm through his, anchoring her safely to his large person.

"Your horse is doing well," he remarked easily.

She had expected him to make some remark on her fall, but his eyes were fixed on the horses. Remembering how Rupert had hated to be distracted when watching a race, she thought he must feel the same, and did not mention her accident. Instead, she answered his comment with a simple, "Yes."

She turned to watch her horse. It was overtaken at the last minute by a showy animal, and the race was over.

"Thought the bay would do it," said Freddy regretfully.

Neither he nor any of the other members of Cassandra's party had noticed her accident.

"Never mind," said Cassandra. "Better luck next time."

"Can I persuade you to join me for some refreshment?" asked Justin. "There is a superior tent at the end, and you are all included in the invitation, of course."

"Thank you," said Maria. "We'd be delighted. Wouldn't we, Harry?"

"Oh, yes," said Harry, receiving a nudge in the ribs. "Delighted."

Cassandra tried to draw her arm away from Justin as they began to walk towards the tent, but he put his hand on top of it and held it firm. The contact was unnerving, awakening the feelings that had been stirred at the soirée. She didn't know why it should be. She glanced sideways at him, taking him in. On the surface he was like any other man of his type, but underneath there was something more. What lay beneath his civilized exterior? she wondered. Because for all his polished manners, there was something dangerous and yet compelling there.

"Did you manage to ask Mr. Goddard everything you wanted to know?" he asked.

"Yes, I did, thank you."

"And?"

"He felt, like you, that it was nothing more than a bad bet."

"Then I hope it has set your mind at rest."

"Yes, it has."

"Good." He smiled down at her. "Now you can forget about it and enjoy the rest of your stay in Brighton."

But it was not so easy. There were still things she wanted to know. Plucking up her courage she began.

"You told me that you were with Rupert on the night he died."

"Yes, I was."

"When I spoke to Mr. Bradley at the soirée, or rather, when he spoke to me, he said I should ask you about the night my brother died. He said . . . he implied . . ."

She did not know how to continue. He walked beside her in silence, not helping her.

She gathered her thoughts, then went on. "He said . . ." She could not reveal what he had really said. *Ask Deverill what he was doing with your brother on the night he died. Ask him what really happened, then see how much you want him to touch you.* But she must know what he had meant. "Lord Deverill, what really happened?"

"I was with Rupert, as Mr. Bradley said. Rupert took a hedge in the dark and unluckily there was a ditch beyond it. His horse fell and he fell with it. He was mortally wounded." His voice dropped. "I am sorry."

Cassandra fell silent. After a time she said, "Mr. Bradley implied there was more."

"Bradley was drunk," he said.

"Yes," she conceded.

"And he was not well disposed towards me."

"No, that's true."

Was there more to the situation? She felt there was, but she also felt that he would say no more. Again she was struck by the layers in him. He was in some ways charming, witty and good company. He was an extremely attractive man, and he made her feel in a way no one had ever made her feel before. But there was something deeper, something darker, hidden away, and the more she learnt about him, the less she felt she knew about him.

They arrived at one of the refreshment tents. Unlike its companions, it was a sedate enclosure, and had none of the drunken behaviour that was going on elsewhere. There were some elegantly dressed people enjoying glasses of ratafia and lemonade, and before long Cassandra found herself seated at a trestle table with a glass of lemonade in front of her. Whilst the others talked of the race, Cassandra continued her conversation with Justin.

"I haven't thanked you yet for saving me," she said. "When I felt myself falling, I feared the worst. It was lucky you'd come up beside me and noticed what was happening, otherwise I would be dead by now. I seem to be accident prone at the moment. I was almost drowned when I went bathing a few days ago, and now I almost fell under a horse! I really need to be more careful. I am not used to mixing with large groups of people, and I have forgotten how to be aware of so many things happening at once. In the country it's very quiet. But I will get used to it again, by and by."

He threw off his drink, then turned towards her.

"You were almost drowned, you say?" he asked casually. "You didn't mention it when I saw you."

"There didn't seem to be any reason to do so. I was bathing, and one of the other ladies was in difficulties. I tried to help her, but she was flailing around so wildly that at last I had to get away from her. I couldn't surface, so I swam under water. When I came up I couldn't see her, so she must have managed to save herself."

He regarded her thoughtfully.

"Not many people can swim under water," he remarked.

"No, but my mother could, and she taught me. She grew up in Brighton, and she was used to the sea. She learnt to swim at an early age. Her parents both felt it was a healthful activity. My grandfather believed in the beneficial properties of sea water. In fact, he believed in them so much that he tried to make my mother drink it. Fortunately, my grandmother said that Dr. Russell might be a great man in some ways, and that he had done them all a great service by turning Brighton into a bathing resort, but that he was a fool for suggesting people drink sea water and that no child of hers was going to drink it!"

He laughed. "That isn't the worst of it. Dr. Awsiter used to recommend that people drink it mixed with milk."

"Ugh!" said Cassandra. "I can think of nothing worse. Fortunately my mother was as sensible as my grandmother, and although she taught Rupert, Lizzie and me to swim, she never made us drink the sea."

"She must have been an unusual lady," said Justin.

"She was." Cassandra smiled as she thought of her mother. "She was advanced in her thinking. She made sure we spent our summers in Brighton so that we could benefit from the sea air, and in the autumn we returned to the estate. She made it seem so easy to organize everything. It wasn't until she died that I realized how difficult it was. She was always singing and cheerful."

She became quiet. He seemed to understand something of what she was thinking, because he said, "It must have been a blow to you when she died."

"Yes." She sighed. "It was. We had no warning of it, you see. She and my father went to London to visit friends. She worried about leaving us behind, but Lizzie was recovering from chicken pox and was too ill to travel and Rupert did not want to go. I was content to stay at home to amuse Lizzie, and so at last she was persuaded to go. We had Moll and John to look after us, as well as a houseful of servants at that time. My mother wrote to us every day. Her letters were cheerful, full of the interesting things she and my father were seeing and doing. Then there was an outbreak of cholera. They were both taken ill, and though their friends nursed them faithfully, they never recovered."

He spoke quietly. "It isn't easy to lose your parents, especially not so young."

There was something in his tone of voice that touched her.

"You sound as though you speak from experience," she said, turning towards him. She saw that his expression had softened. The harsh lines had gone from around his mouth, and his eyes were opaque.

"I do," he said simply. "I, too, lost my parents young, although they did not both die at the same time. My mother died just before I came of age, and my father died a few years later. My mother's death was caused by an old complaint; and my father never recovered from her death. He lost his interest in life and very soon followed her to the grave. I became the guardian of my sister. She was only fourteen at the time. I had an aunt who helped me to give her a season and she married a good man. She is happy now, but it was difficult for her at the time."

"Then we have something in common. My sister, Lizzie, is ten years old. I have tried to be a mother and father to her, but it is not easy."

"It isn't," he said. "You told me she is staying with a friend?"

"Yes, in Hertfordshire." Cassandra smiled. "I had a letter from her yesterday. She's riding and swimming in the river and generally behaving like a hoyden!"

"Has she been to Brighton?"

"Yes. We used to spend the summer here regularly when my parents were alive."

"And now you intend to do so again."

"It would be lovely, but no. I have to try and sell the house. I must do what I can to repair our family's fortunes."

She fell silent, remembering that he, too, must repair his family fortune. A chill breeze blew under the flap of the tent and she drew her shawl more tightly about her. He would marry an heiress. She would sell the town house. And they would never see each other again.

Around them, the others talked.

"I thought my horse was going to win!" she heard Maria saying. "It was doing so well, but after the bend it could not keep up. Even so, I hoped it would make a last minute recovery, but it was mortifying to watch it come in last!" She turned to Cassandra. "I forgot to follow your horse in all the excitement, Cassandra. Did it do well?"

"No. It did very badly. It limped in just before yours," she remarked wryly.

"Didn't have the stamina," said Freddy. "Seen it run before. Mind you, didn't do so well myself. Came in fifth. Dashed queer things, horses. Never know what's going to happen next."

They finished their refreshments.

"I think we should be going," said Maria.

She, Cassandra and Harry took their leave of Justin, whilst Freddy remained behind, talking to Mr. Goddard about the race. As they left the tent, Cassandra felt Justin's eyes on her.

"That was most enjoyable," said Maria, as they emerged on to the Down. "I know Lord Deverill is an attractive man, but he has no fortune," she went on. "He is useful to make you appear sought after, but don't forget that Lord Armington would be a much better husband."

"Lord Deverill has no intention of proposing to me," said Cassandra.

"Oh, good," said Maria.

Cassandra found, to her surprise, that she did not agree. Choosing not to dwell on the unsettling thought, she said,

"Will you help me choose some ribbon?" A major purchase was beyond her, but a small purchase was not. "I want to buy some to trim my new bonnet, and I don't know which colour to choose."

"Of course I will."

The subject of Justin was dropped. The sun was hot, shining down from a clear blue sky. Maria unfurled her parasol and Cassandra went to unfurl hers, only to realize she had left it in the refreshment tent.

"I've forgotten my parasol. I will not be long," she promised Maria. "I will meet you by the ribbon stall."

"Harry will go with you."

"It's all right. I will only be a minute."

She returned to the refreshment tent. As she approached her table she saw that Freddy and Mr. Goddard had gone, but that Justin was still there. He was sitting with his back to her, and next to him was another gentleman. She recognized him as Matthew Standish, the young man who had burst into the room when she had visited Justin's house on her first morning in Brighton. Her eyes drifted over him to her parasol. She was about to move forward and take it, when she heard Matthew say, "You've got to tell her. If she's in danger, she needs to know about it. You can't keep this to yourself."

"No. I can't warn her without telling her everything, and I'm not prepared to do that. I don't want to destroy her peace of mind."

"But if she's had two accidents already, one whilst swimming and one—"

"I can protect her from those."

Cassandra felt a sinking sensation as she realized they were talking about her. Two accidents. A near drowning and a near trampling to death. But what was that Justin had said? That he could protect her? Was that the explanation for his attention to her? Was that why she came across him so often? For some reason, she felt her spirits sinking. She had begun to think it was something more. Her mind flew back to the moment he had kissed her. That had not been prompted by a desire to protect her, at least, and it warmed her to know it.

But Matthew was speaking again.

"No, you can't, Justin. She had one of them whilst swimming, and gentlemen aren't allowed to bathe with the ladies."

"I've already taken care of that; I've set a woman to watch her."

"It isn't enough. You can't let her go through this blind. You have to tell her."

Cassandra felt anxious, but she had to know the truth. "Tell me what?" she demanded.

Justin turned round and his face darkened when he saw her.

"Cassandra, what are you doing here?"

"I forgot my parasol."

She saw him glance round, then his eyes stopped as they fell on her parasol, leaning innocently against one of the benches.

"What do you have to tell me?" she demanded.

"You'll have to tell her now," said Matthew.

But before Justin could reply, a determined voice broke in on him. "Why, if it isn't Lord Deverill! How wonderful to find you here."

Looking round, Cassandra saw Mrs. and Miss Kerrith bearing down on them.

"I was just saying to Eustacie that I thought I'd glimpsed you earlier," went on Mrs. Kerrith. She glowered at Cassandra as she drew level with the table, then turned smilingly to Lord Deverill. "I hope you had better luck with the horses than we did. I do declare, we have had the most dreadful luck. Eustacie's horse refused to run, and mine fell at the first bend.

"Mrs. Kerrith, Miss Kerrith," said Justin, rising and greeting them politely, though to Cassandra it seemed he did so through gritted teeth.

"We were just saying how much we would like some lemonade," said Mrs. Kerrith pointedly. "It is so hot today. Poor Eustacie is quite overcome. But then she is such a delicate flower."

Miss Kerrith looked towards Justin with a wilting air.

His face set in a polite smile. "Then you must allow me to procure it for you. Miss Paxton was just leaving."

Miss Kerrith and her mother gave a satisfied smirk. Cassandra was bitterly disappointed—until Justin handed her her parasol and guided her towards the exit, giving them a few moments alone together.

"I am not leaving the tent until I know what you mean," said Cassandra.

"We can't talk here," he said. "I'm giving a picnic tomorrow, at a scenic spot on the beach. Will you join me? Your friend and her husband are welcome, of course. I will explain everything then."

"I need to know now," said Cassandra.

"Lord Deverill!" called Mrs. Kerrith.

He cursed under his breath. "It's impossible," he said, looking into her eyes. "But I will tell you everything tomorrow. You have my word. I will direct the carriages past your house at eleven o'clock. Be ready to join us."

"Very well," said Cassandra. "We will be there." She hesitated, and then asked, "Am I in danger?"

He took her hand reassuringly.

"Don't worry. There will be people watching you at all times, and no harm will come to you."

She looked into his eyes. "But I am in danger?" she pressed.

He stroked his long, strong fingers across her palm, and she swallowed.

"It's possible," he said.

"Oh, Lord Deverill!" carolled Mrs. Kerrith.

"I must go," he said.

Cassandra nodded.

Then, leaving her, he went back to the Kerriths.

Cassandra walked slowly back to Maria and Harry.

"You found it? Oh, good," said Maria. "The sun is very strong, and it wouldn't do to get freckles. Was Lord Deverill still there?"

Cassandra nodded. "Yes, he was. He has asked us to join him for a picnic tomorrow," she said.

"Oh, good. All the best people go to his picnics. Lord Armington is bound to be there. Now, where were the ribbons you wanted to look at?" asked Maria.

Cassandra roused herself from her thoughts then led the way to a stall displaying fans, stockings, gloves and ribbons. She showed two of the ribbons to Maria.

"Which do you think will go best with my new bonnet, the dark pink or the rose?" she asked.

"The dark pink," said Maria consideringly. "The rose is too insipid."

As Cassandra paid for the ribbon, she found her thoughts straying. Why was she in danger? From whom? And what did Justin have to do with it?

The thoughts haunted her as she returned to the carriage with Maria and Harry. All around, people were enjoying themselves, but for her the world had taken on a darker hue. The hurdy gurdy now sounded tinny and the young ladies who flirted with officers seemed immoral. The pleasure had gone out of her day.

She climbed into the carriage behind Maria, then Harry followed her. The step was folded up and the carriage rolled away.

They left Whitehawk Down behind and bowled down into town.

"I believe I could acquire a taste for the races," said Maria.

"My dear wife, you would ruin us within a month," said Harry.

"Perhaps you are right. I will not bet the next time we go, but will content myself with watching instead."

Listening to their banter, Cassandra wished she could join in, but she could think of nothing but what she would learn on the following day.

CHAPTER SEVEN

Cassandra's thoughts were perturbed as she dressed for the picnic the following morning.

"A picnic?" snorted Moll. "Just you make sure you sit on a blanket, Miss Cassie. I don't hold with this sitting on the grass—it'll be damp, I shouldn't wonder—"

"You needn't worry about that. The picnic is to take place on the beach," Cassandra said.

"Nasty wet places, beaches," said Moll. "You'll catch your death of cold for sure. All this eating out of doors. Why can't people eat inside like sensible bodies? You make sure you wear your shawl, and keep your gloves on. And mind you don't get your feet wet. You'll get your death from wet feet."

"I'll keep them dry," Cassandra promised her.

"And make sure Miss Maria doesn't neither. She was looking tired yesterday. I hope Mr. Harry's taking care of her."

"He is," said Cassandra.

Having grumbled herself out, Moll disappeared to find Cassandra a handkerchief, for if her mistress departed without one then the heavens would surely fall. Cassandra wandered over to the window. As she did so, she saw a footman loitering in the street. The sight would not have interested her the day before but now, knowing that Justin had set a watch on her, she wondered if he was really a footman or if he was a guard in disguise. She felt a chill, and pulled her shawl more tightly about her.

"Don't say as I didn't warn you," said Moll gloomily, as she reentered the room. "You've taken cold. I knew how it would be. Swimming in your chemise, walking along the Downs, mixing with all the rabble at the races . . ."

Cassandra took the handkerchief Moll held out to her and thanked her for it, just as Maria's carriage rolled up. No sooner had it done so than a smart party of carriages arrived behind it. Cassandra put on her bonnet, picked up her parasol and then went outside. She took her place with Maria and Harry, and the group was soon on its way.

It was very different to the group of people who had attended Maria's soirée. They had been comfortable people with incomes large enough to provide them with all the usual luxuries of life, but these people were the most fashionable members of society. Their carriages were the smartest money could buy, a number of them being emblazoned with coats of arms. The ladies were dressed in silk and satin and though their gowns were simple in style, with high waists and long, narrow skirts, they were adorned with the most exquisite lace. Silk parasols with long tassels, bonnets decorated with ribbons and feathers, and gloves dyed in every shade completed their outfits, making Cassandra and even Maria feel positively dowdy.

"I've never seen so many jewels," said Maria to Cassandra in a hushed tone.

"No need to whisper. They can't hear you," said Harry jovially, but even he was impressed with their company.

"What a thing! To be invited to one of Lord Deverill's picnics!" exclaimed Maria. "The weather is perfect. Just look at that sky."

It was an azure blue, with a few fluffy white clouds to break the monotony. From out of it shone a hot sun, made bearable by a cooling breeze.

As they continued on their way. Cassandra's eyes were drawn to the front of the procession, where Justin was riding alongside a carriage full of young ladies.

"The Pargeter girls," said Maria, seeing the direction of her gaze. "There are five of them, all heiresses, and all very handsome. I wonder if Mr. Kingsley will be here today?"

she asked, changing the subject. "He seemed very taken with you."

"I have no desire to marry him, even if he asks me," said Cassandra.

"No, Lord Armington would be the better match," said Maria comfortably.

"My dear wife, I despair of you," said Harry.

They followed the coast for some distance until they reached a sheltered stretch of beach some miles out of town. There were no bathers and no fishermen. They had it entirely to themselves. The sea swooshed as it rushed in, and then retreated with a hissing sound, whilst the gulls cried above.

The servants were soon setting up trestle tables and spreading out rugs and cushions. Cassandra, Maria and Harry walked down to the sea, breathing in the fresh, salty air. The two ladies twirled their parasols to keep the sun off their faces, and Harry picked up a pebble to skim. He threw it across the water and watched it bounce twice before sinking beneath the waves.

"I can do better than that," he said.

He picked up another pebble then discarded it, at last choosing a smooth, flat stone. He rubbed his thumb over it, feeling its shape, then turned sideways to the waves and skimmed it across the sea. One, two, three, four times it bounced before disappearing from view.

"Much better," said Harry.

He bent down for another stone.

Cassandra let her gaze wander over the other guests. There were some thirty people in the party altogether. Some strolled by the water's edge, some sat and gossiped on the rugs, and some were with their children, who were playing at one side of the beach, watched over by nurses and governesses.

It was a peaceful scene, thought Cassandra. The sea was calm, and the ladies looked beautiful as they twirled their parasols to keep the sun off their faces. The gentlemen amused them with light-hearted conversation, and there was an air of bonhomie. The guests were in a mood to please and be pleased. The weather and setting had affected everyone's spirits, and conversation seemed to be flowing easily. If not for the shadow hanging over her, she would have thought the day was perfect.

She glanced towards Justin, but he was busy playing host and she guessed that it would not be until after they had eaten that she would have an opportunity to talk to him. Until then she could not be easy. She was glad that Maria was in a mood to be garrulous, for she could not concentrate well enough to engage in conversation.

"Just wait until I tell Aunt Julia about this!" said Maria. "She will be unbearable. She will brag about it to all her friends. It's so dull for her, living in the remoter reaches of the country, especially now that her hip is troubling her and she cannot get out as much as she used to. But this will enliven her. She has been wanting to find a way of paying Mrs. Jamieson out, ever since Mrs. Jamieson bragged that her niece once entertained a baronet to tea, and this news will be as good as a present for her."

Cassandra let Maria's words wash over her. Harry grew bored of skimming stones and they strolled along the beach before returning to the rest of the group.

To Cassandra's relief, Lord Armington was not one of the party. She did not feel equal to conversing with him, or to fending off Maria's knowing looks.

The footmen had been busy in their absence, covering the tables with white cloths and placing sparkling glasses and abundant silverware on them ready for use. The food was being laid out. Potted mushrooms, artichoke pies and venison pasties were set alongside roasted hams, juicy pheasants and plump capons. There were dishes of buttered crab, dressed lobster and potted shrimps, and potato pudding decorated with puffed pastry. Large pyramids of fruit were arranged as centrepieces and beside them was an array of desserts, with syllabubs, tarts, macaroons and jellies. But Cassandra had no appetite, and Maria's exclamations passed her by.

"This was a splendid notion of Deverill's," said Harry, as they took their places on a large rug. It had been spread out over the beach and then softened with dozens of cushions.

Cassandra agreed.

"There's nothing like eating out of doors," said Maria.

They were joined on the rug by a number of other people, none of whom Cassandra knew. She pulled her thoughts away from Justin and joined in with the conversation.

"May I fetch you something?" asked a gallant young man by the name of Percy Spencer.

"Thank you. I think I'll have a little of the artichoke pie."

"And some capon?" he asked her. "They look very good."

Cassandra thanked him again, and before long found herself with a plate of food on her lap and a glass of champagne in her hand.

"Delicious," said Maria, eating daintily by her side.

Cassandra agreed, but in reality she had little appetite. She could not help her eyes straying to Justin. He was moving amongst his guests, making sure that everyone was comfortable and having an enjoyable time. He glanced at her only once, but then his attention was reclaimed by a dashing dowager.

As soon as she had finished eating, Cassandra declared her intention of taking a walk along the beach. Maria and Harry were feeling too lazy to walk, and Percy had struck up a conversation with another young gentleman, so Cassandra went down to the water's edge by herself. She began to walk beside the sea. The sound of it was soothing. The waves played beside her, forcing her to step away when they came too high, and tempting her to go closer when they ran away, leaving seaweed and small stones in their wake. Ahead of her, a gull waddled across the beach, ducking its head every now and then to peck at something that attracted its attention.

As she went on, the noise of chatter and laughter died away behind her. She did not know how far she had gone until she looked back and found that she had walked round the headland. The picnickers were no longer in sight. She was reluctant to go back, but at the same time she knew she must. She was in danger, Justin had said, and she should not be alone.

She had just taken the first step back when a figure came into view. It was Justin. He continued to walk towards her and then stopped just in front of her.

"At last," he said.

His words were so heartfelt that she knew he had been frustrated by their lack of opportunity to speak as much as she had. He offered her his arm but she declined. She was not sure of herself when she was touching him. Something about him sent her thoughts spiralling down new and uncertain channels, and she did not want the disturbing sensations to distract her.

They began to walk along the coast together.

"I have been trying to talk to you all day, but every time I thought I'd extricated myself, someone else claimed my attention," he said.

"Yes. I saw."

"But now we are alone, and at last we can talk."

"Yes. We can."

She stopped. He said nothing. Then she began. "You said yesterday that I was in danger," she said.

"Yes," he said. "I think you are. Or perhaps it's better to say that I think you might be in danger."

"But I don't understand. Why should I be in danger?" she asked. "Who could possibly want to hurt me?"

He stopped and looked out to sea. "There are some things it is better not to know," he said. "It is better simply to know that you are in danger, and take precautions because of it."

"You're being very mysterious," she said, stopping beside him.

He turned to face her. "I have my reasons."

"Which are?"

"That I would like to protect you, if I can."

She nodded. "You promised Rupert you'd do so." She paused. "When I overheard you talking to Mr. Standish, you said you didn't want to tell me about my danger because you didn't want to destroy my peace of mind."

"That's true. I don't."

"But it has already been destroyed." She met his gaze. "If someone is trying to harm me, then I need to know who it is, and why. It sounds absurd," she went on, looking about her at the peaceful scene. "I cannot understand why anyone would want to do such a thing. I have no enemies. And yet I've had two . . . accidents, for want of a better word . . . and you must have some reason for believing them to be more than that."

"Yes, I have."

She searched his face.

"Whatever it is, I need to know," she said.

"Very well."

"Does it have something to do with my brother?" she asked.

"Why do you ask that?"

"Because he said he had done something terrible. I can find no trace of it, but I think you have been protecting me." She saw by his face that what she had said was true. "If he had done something terrible, then it might explain why I am being attacked. Does it? Does it have something to do with Rupert?

He spoke reluctantly. "I believe so."

"But why? Is it revenge? Did he harm someone, and are they now trying to harm me, as he has passed beyond their reach?"

"No. It is more complicated than that."

He looked down at his boots. He did not want to say more, she could tell, but she had to know.

"I don't know for sure, but I believe someone is trying to kill you because they think you know something that can harm them," he said at last. "I think they suspect that Rupert told you something that would put them in danger."

"What do you mean? What kind of thing? Was there foul play in a race, or something of that kind? Was someone spotted cheating at cards? Did they perhaps win a fortune, and fear that Rupert saw them cheating? Is that, in fact, why Rupert died?" she asked, as the thought hit her. "Did they kill him so that he could not tell anyone what he had seen?"

The thought seemed terrible. And yet, as she saw his swift glance out to sea, she realized the truth was worse. It did not have to do with racing and gambling: it had to do with something far more serious. She felt suddenly afraid. She followed his gaze and looked outwards, over the ocean. On the other side was France, a country that had recently torn itself apart with revolution, and which was now waging war with its neighbours.

"Does it have something to do with the war?" she asked in a whisper.

"Yes, it does. Stop here, Cassandra. I would rather not tell you anything further."

"I can't stop. I have to know."

He searched her eyes, then nodded. "Very well."

He took something out of his pocket. He glanced at it and then handed it to her. She took it and looked at it. It was a print. In the centre of the picture was the English Channel, with France to the left of the picture and England to the right. Over the Channel flew a number of balloons, across it surged a fleet of rowing boats, and under it was a tunnel, with troops moving through it.

"Have you ever seen anything like this before?" he asked.

"Yes. I saw something similar when Rupert came home for a brief visit. He brought it with him. I asked him about it, but he said it was nothing. Just something he'd picked up at a fair."

"It's more than that. It's a plan of action. Not in the details—without a way to steer them, balloons are no threat, and a tunnel under the sea is just a fantasy. But Napoleon's built a fleet of ships, and last year he was ready to invade. Fortunately he did not manage it."

"But you think he will try again?"

"Yes, I do. He has been distracted by other matters recently. There was a plot against his life, and after that he had his coronation to think of, but our intelligence tells us he's still determined to go ahead."

"But what has this to do with me?" she asked, handing the print back to him.

"Nothing, directly. But indirectly . . ."

"It had something to do with Rupert," she said, looking at him for confirmation.

"Yes, it had."

She felt the cold touch of dread. But she had come this far. She would see it through. She waited for him to continue. He did not seem to know how to do it. He walked away from her towards the sea. Then he turned round.

"Napoleon is determined to invade England if he can. But it won't be easy for him. First of all he has to get his ships across the Channel. They're unsuitable, and they won't survive rough weather, but if luck is with him and the weather is fine then they might make the crossing. Then he will have to evade the navy. It's unlikely, but again it's possible. Then he will have to land. There are not many places along the coast that are suitable, and the likely spots are well guarded. Brighton has soldiers camped here, ready to fight any invasion. But if something happened to the soldiers, if their wine was drugged, or if their horses were stolen, or if there was an uprising inland that demanded their presence, or if the camp was set on fire, or if all those things happened together, then the French could land virtually unhindered."

"But that wouldn't be likely to happen—would it?" she asked.

"Yes, it would. Napoleon has paid men and women to

bring about this end. There are traitors in Brighton even as we speak, who mean to make sure the militia are distracted or incapacitated if Napoleon invades."

"But I still don't see what this has to do with me," she said, shaking her head.

"Don't you?" He watched her intently.

"Unless . . . unless you think one of the traitors is trying to kill me," she said. "Is that it? Did Rupert discover something before he died, and the traitors are afraid he mentioned it to me? Their names, perhaps, or some detail of their plans?"

He did not reply.

"I can think of nothing. He never mentioned anything to me. I saw him infrequently, and then he told me about his horses and his clothes. If he had uncovered a plot, I knew nothing about it." She paused. "Do you think it has something to do with his death?" she asked.

She saw his face change. He turned away and walked down to the water. She followed him.

"It does. Tell me what. I must know."

"Cassandra . . ."

He turned to face her again. There was something gentle in his voice, and it frightened her more than a string of curses would have done. She felt a coldness invade her, starting at her extremities and working its way inward towards her heart.

"He had done something terrible," she said in a whisper. "That was what he was talking about in his letter. You told me it was a reckless gamble, and I thought it was an abandoned serving girl, but it was worse, wasn't it?"

"Cassandra . . ."

"Rupert had one of those prints in his pocket." Her voice sounded dead to her own ears. "He was a traitor."

"Cassandra . . ."

"Yes or no. Just tell me, Justin."

He took a step towards her and she took a step back.

"Was my brother a traitor?"

She read the answer in his face.

"Yes," he said. "He was."

"This is terrible. Worse than I'd imagined by far. Oh, Rupert, Rupert . . ."

Justin closed the space between them in one stride and rested his hands on her arms.

She looked down at the ground.

"I'm surprised you can bear to touch me," she said.

"It was not your fault."

"So that is why he wrote to me," she said. "He wanted to confess, but then death overtook him. And his treachery— had that something to do with his death?" she asked, looking at him once more.

He dropped his hands to his side.

"Yes."

She said nothing, needing to make sense of what she had learnt, but she could not make sense of it without knowing more.

"I would like to know what really happened that night," she said.

"I would rather not tell you."

"Please," she beseeched him. "I have to know."

"Very well." His voice had dropped to a low murmur, as though it was an effort for him to speak. "But you will hate me at the end of it."

"No, I could never hate you," she said.

He reached out and cupped her cheek, letting his thumb stroke across the soft skin. She had never felt anything so mesmerizing. She never wanted it to end. She wanted it to go on and on whilst the world disappeared, taking all of its problems with it. She wanted to be standing there with Justin, free and as equals; free to touch him as he was touching her; free to give rein to the feelings that were churning inside her. But then his hand dropped to his side, as though he no longer had the energy to hold it up.

She looked into his face and saw something unbearably sad there. She stopped breathing as it came to her that his touch had not been a caress, it had been a farewell. She was suddenly frightened and opened her mouth to stop him speaking, but it was too late.

"I had been looking for the traitors for many months," he said. "I had helped the government on many occasions, and I gave them my assistance again over this matter. I eventually discovered the names of three of the men I was looking for. I received information as to their whereabouts and I found two of them at a brothel. I handed them over to the proper authorities, and then went in search of the third man—Rupert. One of the women from the brothel ran to warn him. She reached him before me and told him I was coming. By the time I arrived, he had saddled his horse and ridden out of town. I followed. Eventually I caught up with him on the Downs. I gave chase. He took a hedge and landed badly. I followed. I found him lying on the ground, on the other side of the hedge, mortally wounded." His voice dropped. "That is how Rupert died."

Her voice did not seem to belong to her, as she said, "You chased him. That's why he took his horse out at night. Because you were chasing him. And you chased him to his death."

He said nothing, but his face told her everything she needed to know.

She turned away from him. He put his hand on her shoulder, but she was hurt and confused and she did not respond.

"I want to be alone," she said.

"Cassandra—"

"Please."

For a long moment he did not reply. Then he said, "Very well. If that is what you want."

She heard his footsteps crunching across the beach, growing gradually quieter and quieter until they disappeared altogether. She folded her arms round herself, then walked down to the water's edge, but it was not the water she was seeing. It was Rupert. Rupert, dressed in his best clothes on the day he started school; Rupert, making her mother rock with laughter when he impersonated his masters; Rupert helping her father with the horses, grooming them as though they had been his best friends; Rupert tying his first cravat . . . All the memories of childhood welled up inside her and threatened to overwhelm her. And now he was gone, cold and dead, laid in a grave, when he should have had his life before him.

She did not notice the passage of time. It was not until she heard Maria's voice that she was recalled to reality.

"Cassie! Cassie! Oh, I'm glad I've found you."

Cassandra made an effort to shake off the ghosts of the past. She took a deep breath and then turned round to see Maria picking her way across the beach.

"What a wonderful time we've had," Maria said, as she joined Cassandra by the shore. "We are very lucky you met Lord Deverill, Cassie. We would not have been invited on such a picnic otherwise. But I think it's time to go home. The party's breaking up. Why, Cassie," she said, her tone changing as she drew near. "You look terrible. Is anything wrong?"

"No. Nothing. A slight headache," said Cassandra.

"I'm not surprised, it's very hot," said Maria sympathetically. "Oh!" She looked down at Cassandra's feet. "Cassie. You're standing in the water."

Cassandra looked down. Maria was right. She had been so distracted she had not noticed.

"You must have been hot," Maria went on, looking worried. "Are you sure you're all right?"

"Yes. I am. But I'm glad we're going home."

"We will soon be back at the carriage. Harry has ordered it to be brought round."

They went back towards the rest of the party, walking side by side. A number of the picnickers had already left and the beach wore a deserted aspect. The few people who remained were heading for their carriages. The footmen had packed the hampers with the used plates and were folding away the trestle tables. A group of gulls was feasting on the crumbs.

"Ready?" asked Harry, beaming at them.

"Yes, ready. What a wonderful time we've had, and it was all thanks to Cassandra."

Cassandra murmured a reply. As she climbed into the carriage, she saw Justin bidding some of his guests farewell.

He turned his head towards her but, unhappy and confused, she looked away.

"We should thank Lord Deverill," said Maria.

"I've already done it," said Harry. "I thought I'd do it whilst he had a minute to spare."

"A good idea," said Maria. "He's been busy all day. Drive on," she said to the coachman, then yawned. "All that fresh air has made me tired. I'm looking forward to going home."

"So am I," said Cassandra. She leant back against the squabs. She had never wanted to go home so much in her life.

CHAPTER EIGHT

Cassandra passed a restless night and rose with the dawn.
Moll, already awake and busy about the house, brought her
hot water and helped her to dress. Cassandra made a poor
breakfast crumbling her roll and leaving most of it on her
plate, then said "I am going for a walk."

"I'll just get my bonnet," said Moll.

"No," said Cassandra. She wanted to be alone but knew
that with someone trying to kill her, it wasn't wise. Although
Justin had told her he had set someone to watch over her,
she did not want to take a risk of going out unaccompanied.
"I'll take John.

Moll grumbled, but was content to let her mistress go
out in John's charge.

Donning her spencer and bonnet, Cassandra left the

house, but it was not to the sea front or the shops that she went. Instead she turned her steps towards the church where Rupert had been buried. She had not visited it since the day when, just over a year before, she had seen her brother laid to rest.

There was an early morning mist, making everything appear hazy. The sun was partially obscured, but she could feel it would be hot later in the day. She passed a flower seller and bought some flowers, then continued on her way.

As she approached the church, her steps slowed, until she stood outside the lych gate. She rested her hand on the gate. Then she pushed it open and went in. Her brother's grave was at the far end of the graveyard. She walked slowly down the path until she reached it. The gravestone was already showing signs of age. Lichen had started to cover it, softening it and giving it a mellow feel. She knelt down beside it and ran her fingers over the name and dates carved there. Rupert David Charles Edward Paxton. Born 8 January 1780. Died 15 May 1804.

"Oh, Rupert," she whispered. "You were too young to die."

Her feelings were confused. She had begun to like Justin, and to trust him, but how could she ever love him now that she knew he had caused her brother's death?

She looked up in an effort to escape her painful thoughts. Outside the confines of the churchyard, she saw a woman laying flowers on the ground. What is she doing? thought Cassandra. And then she realized. The woman was laying flowers on an unconsecrated grave. Cassandra shivered. She looked back at Rupert's headstone, arranged with the others in the graveyard. Her brother had been given a proper funeral. He had had a church service attended by family and friends. And now he had a proper grave on which she could lay flowers. But would that have been his lot if his treachery had been known? If Justin had spoken of it openly, then the case could have been very different. But he had not. Only he, and a few others, had known of it, and they had protected Rupert after his death. It had been an accident, they had said. He had jumped a ditch and taken a fall.

Some of her pain started to leave her. She did not feel she could see Justin again. It would be disloyal to her brother, but she felt a lessening of her distress.

She laid her flowers on Rupert's grave. As she did so, she realized that Justin and his friends had spoken the truth. Her brother *had* been killed in an accident. He might have been a traitor, and he might have been being pursued, but his death had still been unintentional. Justin had not meant to cause it: he had intended to capture Rupert and nothing more. If only Rupert could have been saved . . . But even as she thought it, she knew it would have been impossible.

She stood up. Walking quietly over to the lych gate, she left the graveyard behind her. John followed at a discreet distance. The mist was beginning to clear and the sun was rising in the sky. It was warm, and the gulls were crying. The sea was calm and unruffled. Fishing boats bobbed gently on its surface. Her own world might have been shaken, but all around her life went on as normal. She found the knowledge soothing, and the tension that had gripped her on learning the truth about Rupert began to disappear, so that by the time she returned to the house, she was ready to face the day.

"I want to sort out the furniture today," she said to Moll, speaking briskly. She knew from experience that hard work could be a solace in times of distress. "Between us, we must take all the spare furniture downstairs to load on to the coach. She turned to John. "I want you to take it back to the estate."

"Yes, miss," said John.

There came a knock at the door.

"It'll be Lord Deverill," said Moll. "He's been here this morning already."

"Tell him I can't see him," said Cassandra.

Moll looked at her in surprise.

Cassandra turned to John.

"Answer the door, John, if you please. Say I am not at home."

John heaved a sigh that said, "Women!" as plain as words, and then left the room.

Moll was not so easily satisifed.

"He's not been trying to take advantage of you, has he?" she asked.

"No, of course not."

"It's not like you to say no to a visitor," said Moll suspiciously.

"I'm too busy for callers at the moment," said Cassandra. "I want to have the house ready for sale by the end of the month. I still have to finish sorting the attic, then I have to help John with the pieces for the estate. I simply don't have time."

"You've time to see Miss Maria," said Moll.

"That's different. Maria's a friend. But Lord Deverill is just making a polite call."

"If you say so," said Moll, though she did not look convinced.

"I do say so," said Cassandra. "Now, we had better see to the furniture."

Moll was silenced.

John soon returned to say that he had sent Lord Deverill away.

"When you take the spare furniture back to the estate, I think I will come with you," said Cassandra to John. "I will need to arrange it when we get there. Some of it is good enough to go downstairs. Other pieces will go in the spare bedrooms."

"Very good, miss," said John.

Cassandra felt her spirits begin to lift. The idea of a few days in the country was very appealing to her. It would give her a chance to rest and refresh her spirits somewhat before returning to Brighton.

"I have promised Maria I will go and see Granmere Park with her on Monday, but then I have no more engagements for a week. We will set out on Tuesday. You will stay here, Moll. I need you to look after the house whilst I'm away."

"Very good, miss," said Moll. "And a good thing, too," she muttered. "The springs on that coach aren't what they used to be."

"Make sure the coach is ready when I need it," said Cassandra to John.

"Don't you worry, Miss Cassie. It'll be ready," said John.

~ ~ ~

Justin stood by the fireplace in his drawing-room, his hand in his waistcoat pocket. It was now two days since the picnic and his efforts to see Cassandra had been in vain. He had wanted to explain to her, to tell her the full story, but she would not give him the chance. There was more she had to know, and it might help to ease her pain.

He remembered how badly he had wanted to comfort her, on the seashore. He remembered how warm she had felt when he had put his hand on her shoulders. He had wanted to take her in his arms, but she had withdrawn from him, telling him she wanted to be alone.

And now she had refused to see him. He found he could not blame her. It had been his duty to chase Rupert, but he could not expect her to see it that way, because he had been the cause of her brother's death.

He looked at the locket again. He had meant to return it to her after Rupert's death. He had meant to give it to her again when he had discovered she was in Brighton, but he hadn't been able to part with it. And now he knew he never would.

~ ~ ~

Cassandra finished sorting out the spare furniture and by the time Monday arrived she felt she could join Maria in a tour of Granmere Park with an easy conscience. Her work in Brighton was almost done. When she dressed, she did so more warmly than previously, wearing a long-sleeved gown and donning a pelisse instead of a short spencer. The weather had turned cooler, and it looked as though it might rain.

"I am looking forward to seeing Granmere Park," said Maria, as they set out together, accompanied by Harry. "I hear it is wonderful."

The carriage rolled through the streets of Brighton and then made its way out into the country, bowling through winding lanes. The fields and hedgerows were yellow and needed a downpour to restore their fresh, rich green.

After an hour of travelling they reached a massive set of gates and went in, arriving in front of a splendid Palladian villa soon afterwards. It glowed in the blue light as the sun shone down on it through heavy clouds. A terrace stretched in front of it, and steps led up to the door.

"Are you sure it's all right for us to visit like this?" asked Cassandra.

"Positive," said Maria. "Harry and I do it all the time. As long as the owners are not at home, they are happy for their housekeepers to show people round. I have it on good authority that Lady Anne is visiting friends."

The footman let down the step and they climbed out of the carriage, then went up the steps to the front door. The footman knocked. The door was opened by an elderly butler, and on stating their business he bade them welcome and sent for the housekeeper.

Cassandra was relieved. It seemed that Maria was right about visits being commonplace.

The housekeeper soon joined them in the imposing hall. She was a sensible looking woman, soberly dressed in a grey gown.

"It's a splendid house," said Maria.

"That it is," said the housekeeper. "I've seen many fine houses, but none to compare with Granmere Park. Lady Anne and her husband have done a great deal to improve it since they bought it a few years ago."

"It is not their ancestral home?" asked Maria.

"No. Lady Anne fell in love with it, and her husband is always pleased to give her anything that will make her happy. The marble columns are some of the finest in the country," said the housekeeper, directing their attention to the finest feature of the hall.

Cassandra could well believe it. They were very impressive.

"The floor, too, is made of marble."

The housekeeper went on to point out the sweeping staircase and to comment on each of the works of art adorning the walls.

Having displayed the hall, she took them through into the morning-room, which was no less splendid. The proportions were elegant, and it was adorned with plasterwork. She then took them into the other principle rooms, leading them in to a huge gallery.

"This is part of the original house, which was built in Elizabethan times."

"The house has been rebuilt then?" asked Maria.

"Yes. The first house was almost destroyed by a fire."

"There are no portraits," said Harry in surprise.

"No. Lady Anne has had the gallery remodelled and she is going to oversee the hanging of the family portraits personally when she returns."

The housekeeper proudly related the house's history as she continued the tour, until at last she took them into the drawing-room, where the tour ended.

It was a beautiful room. The arched windows stretched almost from floor to ceiling, giving magnificent views of the parkland beyond.

"These are some of the best views in the house," she said. "From here you can see the lake."

Cassandra, Maria and Harry admired the view.

"Is it possible to see the grounds?" asked Maria, looking out of the window. The sky was grey, but there was no rain.

"Of course. They were landscaped by Capability Brown, and they are a fine example of his work. I'll arrange for one of the gardeners to guide you. There is a very fine walk round the lake."

Cassandra and Harry expressed themselves pleased with the idea, and they were soon outside. Lawns ran away from the house, inviting the eye to follow them. Vistas were created between arrangements of trees, and the whole was spacious and pleasing to the eye.

"You'll be wanting to see the lake," said the gardener, when they had admired the trees and lawns.

"Yes, please," said Maria.

The gardener led them down to the water. Maria walked slowly and, without realizing it, Cassandra moved ahead. Before long she had outstripped them entirely, and when she looked back she found that they were lost to view. Deciding she must wait for them to come into sight, she went over to the edge of the lake. It was grey, reflecting the lowering sky, and reeds grew around the edge.

A ripple broke the water, then another and another. It was starting to rain. Soft spots fell slowly to begin with, then became more frequent, until at last it was in danger of turning into a torrent. She was about to turn back when she saw a lodge by the water's edge a little further on. The sky was darkening with every passing second, and at any minute the rain could come pelting down. If she tried to return to the house she would be soaked, so she ran towards the lodge and went in, shaking the water out of her eyes as she closed the door behind her.

By the look of it the lodge was used as a store. There were oars and fishing rods on the floor, together with nets and rowlocks. There were some shelves on the wall, with an assortment of clutter on them, and in the corner there was a rickety chair. She took out her handkerchief and dusted it, then sat down.

The rain came down heavily outside, bouncing on the roof. She wondered if Maria and Harry would head towards the lodge or whether they would go back to the house. As if in answer to her question, the door began to open.

"Isn't this weather dreadful?" she said. And then stopped. For the person coming through the door was not Maria or Harry. It was Justin.

She sprang up in astonishment. "What are you doing here?"

"Cassandra." He looked as astounded as she was. "I did not expect to see you here," he said.

"I was visiting the house with Maria and Harry. We were touring the grounds when it came on to rain. Maria has a passion for old houses," she explained.

"Ah. It's a very fine house. My sister lives here. She has been away, but she will be returning later today. I have brought her hound back for her. I left him at the house and came down to the lake, but then I was caught in the rain."

"I had not realized your sister lived here," she said. "Maria did not tell me the name of the owners. But of course, that would not have let me know either."

"No. My sister has married."

An uncomfortable silence fell.

"I must go," she said.

"It's raining," he said.

"I believe it's stopping."

"It's falling as heavily as ever," he said. "Cassandra—"

She cut him off. "I have to go."

"No. Not until you've heard me out. I've been trying to see you, but your butler has kept insisting that you are not at home."

"I have been busy."

"But you are not busy now."

"Lord Deverill—"

"Cassandra, I know you despise me but—"

"No. I don't despise you."

His mouth relaxed a little, and some of the tension left his large body.

"You don't?"

"No." Her eyes raised to meet his. "But I can't stay," she said.

"You have to. At least until you have heard what I have to say. You haven't heard everything. There is more you need to know."

"I don't think I can stand any more," she said in a low voice.

"It is better," he said. "Things are not as bad as you think. I tried to tell you before, but you were too distressed. I tried to visit you to explain, but you wouldn't see me. Now you must hear me out. You owe it to Rupert."

"Very well," she said reluctantly.

"Won't you sit down?" he said.

She resumed her place on the seat, and he stood before her. He ran his hands through his wet hair. Then he said, "That night . . . the night of Rupert's death . . . you know that he was a traitor and that I was chasing him. You know that he confessed his guilt to you, but what you don't know is that he did everything in his power to undo the harm he had done. When he fell, when he knew that he was dying, he told me he was glad I had caught him. He had never meant things to go so far. He had been drawn in, gradually to begin with, and then more and more deeply, until he had not known how to get out. He told me that he bitterly repented what he had done, and he offered me the names of the other men involved in the treachery, in exchange . . ." His voice caught, then he continued. "In exchange for my promise to help you, should you need it."

"Ah. So that is why you made the promise."

"Yes."

"And did you catch the other traitors?" she asked.

"I did. All except one. Rupert didn't know the name of the man who had organized them."

"Then he is still at large."

"He is. What is worse, I think he—or she—suspects you know something, and that is why you have been attacked."

She looked at the floor. There was a pool of water round her feet, and she remembered Moll's tirade when she had returned from the picnic with wet feet. She moved them to the side, putting them on dry boards.

She sat thinking, then said, "It doesn't make sense. If the ringleader wanted me dead, why did he not try to kill me before?"

"Because you were buried on your country estate, where you were no threat to anyone. But then you came to Brighton. Even worse, you started talking to Rupert's friends about a letter in which he had said he had done something terrible. I tried to persuade you to abandon the quest but, when you refused, I warned his friends so that they would not let anything slip. I made sure you found them very easily so that you could speak to them as quickly as possible and then abandon the subject."

She folded her arms around herself. She was cold.

He sat down beside her, and she did not move away.

"I did not want to tell you all this," he said. "I wanted to protect you without you knowing it. But you guessed too much, and then it was better that you knew everything. I'm sorry," he said. "I wish I could have spared you."

She gave a deep sigh.

"It is not your fault. I loved my brother deeply, but he was always weak. If we had not lost our fortune then I'm sure he would not have turned traitor, but he felt it hard. He wanted the life of a gentleman, but my father's investments failed and we were reduced to living within straitened means. It meant Rupert could not go to university with his friends. He could not have all the things he had grown up wanting. That is why he went to Brighton, I'm sure. It is cheaper to cut a figure here than in London, and he was always fond of luxurious living. If he was offered money, and an easy way to get it, I don't think he would have asked too many questions. I don't believe he would have betrayed his country knowingly, at least not to begin with, but if someone had asked him to carry messages and offered him a great deal of money for doing so, he would have been too deeply involved to draw back."

"Yes, that was the way of it. He did not know what he was doing at first. He was approached by a man named Carstairs—one of the men I caught on the night of Rupert's death—and asked to invite certain men to his next carouse. It was a simple enough thing to do, and he was offered a large sum of money for doing it. He knew he was doing something wrong, because he would not have been offered such a large sum of money otherwise, but he thought he was providing a safe meeting house for smugglers. He did not know he was entertaining traitors. It was not until later that he discovered what he was doing, and by then he was too deeply involved to get out. They would have killed him if he'd tried." He looked her in the eye. "Do you resent me for it? Your brother's death?"

"No. I did to begin with, but you couldn't know he would fall from his horse. You had to stop him and those he worked for. If not, Napoleon could have invaded. And in a way I am grateful to you. You protected his name after his death. You could have revealed his treachery, but you didn't. You made sure he had a dignified funeral."

His eyes lost their harrowed look, and he relaxed. Until that moment she had not realized how tense he had always been when near her. Now, finally, she understood why.

"Did you really think I would hate you for it?" she said softly.

"Yes, I did."

"And . . . and that mattered to you?" she asked hesitantly.

"Yes, it did."

He turned towards her. He lifted his hand as though he was going to touch her, but then he let it fall.

"Cassandra, I want you to go back to your estate," he said. "You're in danger whilst you remain in Brighton. If you had suffered one accident, it would have been suspicious, but you have suffered two, and I am sure someone is trying to take your life."

"It all seems incredible," she said with a shudder.

"Believe me, the danger is very real. Will you at least think about it? Not only for your sake, but for your sister's."

"I was planning to return for a few days anyway."

"Good."

"The danger is real, you say?"

"Yes. Very real."

"Then I'm worried about Lizzie. If anything happens to me . . ."

"It is not her fault that she has been caught up in all of this. If any harm befalls you, you may rest assured I will make her my ward."

"Thank you. That means a great deal to me."

"But nothing is going to happen to you. Cassandra—"

She turned up her face to his.

"Yes?"

He was about to speak, and then appeared to think better of it, because bending towards her he tried to kiss her softly on the forehead, but she turned away, confused.

"Cassandra!" came a voice, breaking the moment.

"It's Maria," she said. "I must go."

He nodded. "You will remain on your estate until I have found out who is responsible for attacking you?" he asked.

"Yes," she said. "I will."

She did not like the idea of being driven out of Brighton, but she could not risk her life whilst Lizzie had no one else to rely on. She knew that Justin would keep his word if anything happened to her, but the little girl needed more than a guardian. She needed a family, and Cassandra was all the family she had left.

"I think you should go first thing tomorrow morning," he said.

"Very well. Do you think I will be followed?"

"No. I will make sure you are not," he said.

She was surprised at his uncompromising tone, but then reminded herself that he had spent years working for the government on dangerous endeavours, and that this sort of situation was not unknown to him. She was still learning things about him, which added to her confused feelings, which alternately drew her towards him then pulled her back.

She walked over to the door, then turned back. "Will you catch the ringleader?"

"Yes. We will. We've narrowed down our search and are closing in on him—or her. We have a list of a dozen names. It's only a matter of time before we catch whoever it is."

"And you will let me know if you catch them, so that I may return?"

"Yes, I will."

She nodded, then opened the door and went out. Justin followed her. The rain had stopped, all but for a last few spots, and the sky was beginning to clear.

"I think it will be better if we don't walk back together," she said.

"Very well."

She heard Maria's voice again and began to walk towards it, but Maria was much closer than she had thought, and quickly came into view.

"There you are. We thought we had lost you." Maria's

eyes moved to Justin. "Lord Deverill!" she said in surprise.

"Lord Deverill's sister owns the house," said Cassandra. "We met whilst walking round the lake."

"Oh!" said Maria.

"Have you enjoyed your visit?" asked Justin, covering the awkward moment with a pleasantry.

"Yes, thank you, it's a fine house. A very fine house."

"Good. I'm glad you think so. My sister will be pleased. Nothing gratifies her more than to know that other people appreciate it!"

They began to walk back towards the stables, talking of the splendour of the mansion. They had almost reached the end of the lawn when a young woman rounded a corner of the house ahead of them. She was small and dainty, and was dressed in a bewitching carriage-dress of amber muslin with a matching pelisse. Yellow gloves formed a fashionable contrast, and a Roxborough hat adorned her dark curls. Behind her trotted Troilus, looking very pleased to have his mistress home again.

"Justin! They told me at the house that you were here! What a welcome surprise. You must stay to tea and tell me all about Troilus. Did he behave himself—Oh!" she went on, catching sight of the rest of the party. "You have guests." Her eyes ran over Cassandra, Maria and Harry, and then returned to Cassandra. "How very charming. You must all stay to tea."

"It's very kind of you, but we mustn't inconvenience you," began Cassandra, sensing a feeling of constraint coming from Justin. And small wonder, for the atmosphere between them was far from easy.

"It's no inconvenience. I insist. It isn't often I have unexpected visitors, and as Justin will tell you, I love surprises."

"If you're sure it's no trouble," said Maria, delighted.

"None at all. Quite the reverse. I have been longing to show someone the new chimney piece in the dining-room, and now I will be able to do so. We don't show the dining-room to casual visitors, but it is one of the best rooms in the house."

"Thank you. We'd be delighted," said Harry.

The five of them turned and walked back to the house together.

"You must allow me to introduce you," said Justin, his attitude becoming less constrained. "My sister, as always, has run on, without a thought for the conventions."

He spoke with a smile which took any sting out of the words.

"I confess, I had quite forgotten," she said with a dimple.

"Might I present my sister, Lady Anne Carmarthon. Mr. and Mrs. Winter, and Miss Paxton."

The introductions over, Anne said, "Now tell me, Justin, did Troilus behave himself?"

"In a manner of speaking," said Justin.

Anne looked at him questioningly.

"He hid my cravat, chewed my best boots and horrified the Duchess of Loomonth by licking her face."

"The Duchess invariably wears too much powder, and it must have offended Troilus's sense of what was proper," said Anne with a saucy smile.

Justin laughed.

In his sister's company, at least, he could be relaxed, thought Cassandra. Listening to their light-hearted banter, she caught a glimpse of his family life. His sister obviously trusted him and loved him very much. Anne had been left in his care as a young girl, and had gone on to become a happy woman, and she hoped that she could do as well by Lizzie.

She turned to look at Justin. His face had lost its strained lines and become open and carefree. He looked younger, and his smile was appealing. He was a different man away from state problems, and she found herself wishing they had met in happier circumstances. Then she might have seen more of his lighter side.

"But you have not been looking after him properly," Anne continued as they walked towards the house. "He looks overfed. You must have been giving him titbits. Either that, or not walking him enough."

"It has nothing to do with that, and everything to do with the string of sausages he stole from the breakfast-table yesterday," remarked Justin.

"A likely story! Justin always overfed the dogs, even as a boy," said Anne confidingly.

"I can rely on my sister to destroy my reputation with anyone she meets," he remarked.

"Of course. That's what sisters are for," she teased him.

"As long as you accuse me of nothing worse than over-feeding the dogs, I will be content."

"I will say nothing more. Of the time you took father's horse when he had expressly forbidden you to ride it I will say nothing. And talk of how you climbed on to the roof, pretending it was the turret of a castle, and then fell off and broke your arm will never cross my lips. Nor will I embarrass you by telling everyone how you rescued my doll when Cousin William threw her into the lake."

It began to rain again and they hurried into the house. Footmen helped them remove their outdoor clothes and then Anne led the way into the dining-room.

"Oh!" said Maria.

"Do you like it?" asked Anne.

"It's wonderful," said Maria, going over to the chimney piece and admiring the intricately carved marble.

"Don't encourage her," said Justin fondly.

"I was so pleased when we found this house," said Anne. "It had become very run down, and my husband and I have spent the last three years restoring it. This is my favourite room."

Cassandra could see why. It was a large apartment, with high ceilings and elegant proportions. Decorated in shades of pale green, it had white plasterwork on the walls and ceiling, and the furniture was Louis XVI. Its graceful lines complemented the graceful proportions of the room. An Aubusson carpet covered the floor, adding an air of restrained luxury to the room.

After bidding them sit down, Anne rang for tea.

"How did you enjoy your stay in London?" Justin asked Anne.

"Well enough, but it was really too hot. Have you been to the capital, Miss Paxton?" she asked.

"Yes," said Cassandra. "Not very often, but on occasion."

"Aren't the shops wonderful?"

"Yes, they are."

"I visited Ackermann's showrooms, and of course I went to Grafton House. Charles swears he will not go to Grafton House with me again, as I spent four hours there examining all the fabrics. I declare, it only felt like four minutes to me."

"How is Charles?" Justin asked.

"Very well. He is coming home tomorrow. I like to arrive first," she said to Cassandra. "Then I can have everything ready by the time he gets here."

"Have you read any more of Mrs. Radcliffe's novels?" asked Cassandra.

She looked from Cassandra to Justin in surprise.

"I came across Miss Paxton on the way to the library and we exchanged our views on the latest novels. I told her you were fond of Mrs. Radcliffe's books."

"I see. No, I have not read anything by Mrs. Radcliffe recently, but I have just read Maria Edgeworth's *Belinda.*"

"I haven't read that," said Cassandra. "I have just finished *Castle Rackrent.*"

"Oh, that is much better. It is one of my favourites. Did you like it?"

"Yes, I did. My only complaint is that it is too short."

"That is exactly what Justin said! But it is still a very good book. I like it almost as much as *Udolpho.*"

They talked of books until tea was brought in, comparing the different Brighton libraries and discussing their favourite novels. The butler and footmen carried in everything necessary on a succession of trays and Anne presided.

"Do you play at cards?" she asked Cassandra afterwards.

"Yes."

"Oh, good. I am a terrible player, but Justin likes to play. This table is perfect for cribbage," she said, pulling a table forward and taking out a deck of cards. She turned to Maria and Harry. "I hope you will indulge me by telling me what I have missed in Brighton whilst I have been away."

"Of course," said Maria.

Harry added his assent.

"You must forgive my sister," said Justin.

"Not at all," said Cassandra, not wanting to betray her feelings.

In truth, she scarcely understood them herself. She should not feel pleasure in his company, and yet she did. Confusingly, she also felt pain. There was no denying that her life had become difficult since meeting Justin, but she would not have foregone their meeting, even if she could have done.

"Will you go first?" he asked.

"Yes."

He dealt the cards and they began to play. Justin was a good player, but Cassandra had the satisfaction of beating him. Her luck did not hold, however, and she lost their next game. A third game would have decided it, but as Justin began to shuffle the cards the clock on the mantelpiece chimed the hour.

"We must be going," said Maria, standing up.

Cassandra glanced at the clock, and was surprised to see that two hours had passed. The visit had been far longer than was generally acceptable, but Anne did not seem to mind.

"I have been so glad to meet you," she said. "I hope you will do me the honour of attending my ball the week after next."

"That's very kind of you," said Maria. "Harry and I would be delighted."

"I hope you, too, will come," said Anne to Cassandra.

Faced with a direct invitation, Cassandra did not feel she could refuse. To her surprise, she did not mind. The afternoon had done much to dispel the awkwardness she had felt in Justin's company. She had enjoyed talking to him and playing with him, discovering a companionableness that she had not expected.

"Good," said Anne. "Then it is settled."

The carriage was brought round. Cassandra took her place beside Maria and opposite Harry, and the coach rolled away.

"Well, I did not expect that," said Maria with satisfaction.

"Nor I," said Cassandra, thinking of her surprising day.

"And to crown it all, an invitation to a ball."

"Yes."

Cassandra could not decide whether she was looking forward to the ball or not. It would be difficult in some ways, and yet her spirits rose when she thought about it.

"We must spend the next few days shopping," said Maria. "I need some new lace for my dress, and I am sure you need something, too."

"I will not be here for the next few days," said Cassandra.

"Not here?" asked Maria in surprise. "What do you mean?"

"I am taking the spare furniture back to the estate. I don't want it cluttering up the house when I try to sell it."

"Oh, I see. Can John not see to it?"

"It's not fair to expect him to do it alone. Besides, he will not know where to put everything. I have not decided myself. If I go with him, I can sort it out before returning."

"But you will not be gone for too long?"

"No, I hope not."

"Then we will go shopping when you come back." Maria hesitated, then said, "I should not tell anyone you are going away, Cassie. If you do, you will have to tell them why, and it is better not to let everyone know you are poverty stricken. There's no need to mention selling the house until you are absolutely certain you are going to do so."

"Some people seem to know about it already. It's difficult to prevent such news leaking out."

"Even so, there is no need to advertise it."

Cassandra agreed, but for very different reasons. The fewer people who knew she was leaving Brighton, the better.

"Very well," she said.

She found herself hoping that Justin would be able to find the traitors' ringleader quickly so that she could return to Brighton and finish her business. And she could not disguise from herself the fact that she was looking forward to Anne's ball.

~ ~ ~

Anne and Justin remained in the drawing-room when their guests had gone. Anne was sitting on an elegant chaise-longue looking through a fashion journal, whilst Justin stood by the mantelpiece, winding the clock.

Anne turned over the pages of a fashion journal, then said nonchalantly, "I like her."

"Who?" Justin asked.

"My dear brother, don't try to dissemble," she said, putting the journal down on her knee. "It doesn't become you. Besides, it does no good. You have never been able to fool me."

"I don't know what you're talking about," he returned, setting the clock straight again.

"I'm talking about Cassandra."

He raised one eyebrow. "Do you mean Miss Paxton?"

"No. I mean Cassandra. I think you should marry her."

"This is very sudden," he said lightly. "You've only just met her. Besides, you told me not six weeks ago that I should marry Miss Kerrith."

"That was different."

"In what way?"

"You had just celebrated your thirtieth birthday, and as

no one had caught your eye, I thought you should marry the first suitable young lady you came across. Miss Kerrith was a good choice. She was pretty, not too spoilt, and best of all, an heiress. I know you loved Papa. So did I. But he had no head for business, and when his investments failed he ran up ruinous debts. I hated to see you sell the estate. I hated it even more when you had to sell your hunters in order to give me a season."

"How did you know about that?" he asked in surprise.

"I heard the servants talking. I have always known what you sacrificed for me so that I could have a splendid come out and I've always been grateful for it. It enabled me to meet Charles, and I have been very happy with him, but now I'd like the same happiness to befall you. If you marry Cassandra I think it will."

"She's very charming, but I prefer brunettes," he said lightly.

She laughed. "Oh, no, Justin, that won't do. I know exactly how you feel about her. Why else would you keep her portrait in your pocket? And not just any pocket, but the one right over your heart."

"What?"

"It's in a gold locket, on a slim gold chain. How you came by it I don't know, but I do know that you are never parted from it."

"How did you know about it?" he asked in amazement.

"My dear Justin, it was not difficult. I saw you fiddling with it so many times that I wondered what you could keep in your waistcoat. At last my curiosity overcame me, and I slipped into your room whilst you were taking a bath."

He gave an exclamation and threw up his hands in a mixture of disgust and despair.

She looked at him intently.

"You're angry with me," she said.

He walked across the room and stood looking down at her.

"No, I'm not angry with you. I could never be angry with you. But I would rather you didn't mention this to anyone else."

"Of course not, if you don't want me to." She paused, then said, "It is serious, then?"

"No, it is not. Miss Paxton will never marry me."

"That is not what I mean. Your feelings for her are serious?"

"Yes, they are. But it's hopeless," he said with a sigh.

"You seem very sure about that," she remarked, eyeing him intently.

"I am."

"It is surely worth asking her?"

"No. It's impossible."

"It seems perfectly easy to me," she rallied him.

He shook his head. "You don't understand."

"Then explain it to me."

He shook his head.

"There are some things I cannot explain, Anne, even to you."

She regarded him for a few moments, then said, "Very well, if you can't, you can't. But I would like to see you married, all the same, Justin."

He gave a twisted smile.

"If I am lucky, maybe Miss Kerrith will have me."

She didn't smile at his forced banter. Instead, she looked troubled.

"I wish I knew what has happened to you recently. You are not usually like this. You usually set out to get the things you want in life, and you usually succeed. I know you want Cassandra, it's no use denying it, but for some reason you won't pursue her. Why not? Has something happened between you? Is that it?"

"Anne—"

"Is it something very bad?" she asked.

He turned towards her, revealing the hurt in his eyes.

"Yes, my dear, I'm afraid it is."

"In time . . ." she said hesitantly.

"No. Not in time. I did something to hurt her, unwittingly, and it goes too deep." He remembered the way she had turned from him when he had tried to kiss her on the forehead. "She has forgiven me for it and in time, perhaps, we might have become friends, but even that is no longer possible. She means to sell the Brighton house and retire to her estate. Once the summer is over, I will not even have the comfort of seeing her."

Anne put her hand on his arm, then said, "She is coming to my ball in two weeks' time. A lot can happen in two weeks."

Justin smiled. But to himself, he thought, *That is exactly what I'm afraid of.*

CHAPTER NINE

〜◎〜

Cassandra set off early the following morning, before fashionable Brighton was astir. The coach rolled through the streets and out of town. The fields were fresh under the early morning sky, with dew still clinging to the grass. After the blue of the sea, it was refreshing to be surrounded by green fields again.

They stopped once, at an inn, where they partook of a light luncheon, and then pressed on, reaching her house late in the afternoon. She felt a surge of happiness as the coach rolled in between the stone gateposts and went up the drive, turning a last bend to reveal her much-loved home.

It was a gentleman's residence of ample proportions, and from a distance there was no sign of decay. Two storeys tall, it had large windows arranged symmetrically along the front. There was a small parapet concealing the bottom of the hipped roof, and there were windows set into the roof. They shed light on the servants' quarters, although the quarters were now empty. The servants had gone, and only Moll and John remained. Because of their age and their position as friends as well as servants, Moll and John did not sleep in the attic, but both slept on the first floor.

As the coach rumbled between the wide lawns, Cassandra decided she must do something about the grounds. The flowerbeds under the windows were overgrown and untidy. The Paxtons had never been gardeners and Cassandra was no exception, being unable to tell a plant from a weed, but she resolved to ask Mrs. Windover, the rector's wife, for instruction. It would be cheerful to have colourful flower beds in front of the house to brighten it.

The coach came to a halt and Cassandra alighted. The house might be run down and heavily mortgaged, but it was home. She unlocked the door and went inside. It was just as she had left it, with its oak panelling glowing in the late summer sunshine, and its moth-eaten carpet swirling with motes of dust. The long-case clock ticked companionably in the corner, and the oak table pushed against the wall creaked in welcome as she set down her valise. The stairs rose ahead of her, their ancient steps worn in the middle by countless generations of Paxton feet.

Cassandra took off her bonnet and spencer and went into the library, where the mixture of grandeur and shabbiness continued. The furniture was a blend of solid oak and more modern, gilded pieces, but most of the gilding was coming off. The curtains were made of heavy damask, but they had been attacked by moths. The Aubusson carpet was threadbare and the porcelain ornaments were chipped. But the bookcases had been lovingly polished, and the leather books on the shelves filled the air with their scent.

She wandered over to the window. The wide lawns, kept short by Farmer Jenkins' sheep, stretched away to a shrubbery beyond. It seemed impossible to believe that, only a few days ago, someone had been trying to kill her. Now that she was at home again, the idea seemed fantastic. Might not her accidents have been simply accidents? An accidental dipping was not uncommon and could easily be accounted for. Then, too, the race track had been crowded. Might she not have been jostled by a fellow race-goer who had had no intention of knocking her under the hoofs of the horses?

But then there was Rupert . . . He had been a traitor. And if Justin was worried, she would do well to be worried, too.

Rupert. Her thoughts went to her brother. What was it Mr. Elwin had said? She thought of the man who had insulted her at the assembly rooms, by suggesting she become some man's mistress. "He was always fond of money." Yes, he had always been fond of money. Too fond. When they had played their game of buried treasure in their childhoods, she had always wished for a new gown and Lizzie had wished for a doll, but Rupert's wishes had been more extravagant. He had wished for a pair of matched bays, then four matched bays, then a string of racehorses, then a hunting lodge, then a house in London . . . the list had gone on. Rupert's fondness for money had been his downfall.

As she thought of Mr. Elwin, Cassandra found herself wondering if he could be the traitors' ringleader. There had been something dissolute about him, and he had known Rupert. He might have decided to exploit Rupert's love of money. And if not him, who? Peter Raistrick? He seemed like a nice young man, but there had been something about him that hadn't quite rung true. Or Geoffrey Goddard? It wasn't pleasant to think that one of those men might have tried to kill her, but she must not discount the possibility that they were more than they seemed.

She cast her mind back to the race track. She had seen Mr. Goddard there, but she had not noticed Peter Raistrick or Mr. Elwin. It had been crowded, though, and she might not have spotted them.

But this was absurd, she told herself. They might have

pushed her on to the track but they could not have tried to drown her. They were men, and men and women bathed separately. Unless they had paid someone to do it . . . Or unless the traitors' ringleader was a woman, someone she had not thought of. Possibly someone she had not met . . .

She thought back to the day when she had gone bathing. If only she had been able to see who had pushed her under the water, but she had been floating on her back at the time she had first been knocked beneath the waves, and after that, she had been too busy trying to save herself to look at her attacker. Besides, in their voluminous gowns and bathing hats, most people looked the same. Except . . . She frowned in concentration. As an arm had flailed wildly past her face, she had caught sight of a small mole on her assailant's wrist. It probably meant nothing. The person who had attacked her could have been hired to do so, and she might never see them again. Even so, it would be useful in identifying them should they ever be caught.

"Where shall I put the drum table?" asked John, rolling a mahogany table awkwardly into the room.

"In the drawing-room, I think, John. It just needs a new caster, and then we can use it."

"Very good, miss"

Putting aside her speculation, Cassandra helped him to sort and arrange the furniture. She was home again now. She did not have to worry about being attacked any more.

Instead, she had to worry about walking into the village and buying something for them to have for their supper.

~ ~ ~

Three days later, Cassandra had still not heard from Justin. She had hoped he might have caught the villain by now, but she was not too downhearted. She had no need to be in Brighton for the present, and whilst she was at home she had plenty to do. She had been so busy, in fact, that she had forgotten all about the letter she had received from Lizzie just before going to visit Granmere Park. She had put it in her reticule, meaning to read it as soon as she had time, but events had driven it out of her mind. Now that she was at leisure she remembered it and began to read.

> *Darling, darling Cassie,*
> *I am having a wunderul time. I don't want it to end. Can Jane come and stay with us? She will be very good and not eat much becos she knows we don't have any munny. Darling Cassie, you must let her come becos if not she will have to go and see her great grandmother who likes to kiss peeple which Jane says is HORRID becos her great grandmother has a mustash. Please, darling Cassie, rite to Jane's mama and say she can come and stay with us, PLEASE . . .*

Cassandra laughed as she read the letter. On finishing it, she took up her quill and began to write.

Dear Lizzie,
Yes, Jane can come and stay with us. I will write to her mama and say how happy we would be to have her with us.
Your spelling grows worse. I can only hope you pay more attention to it at the seminary, otherwise I will be receiving a stern letter from your teachers. I think I will have to make you practise when you return home.

She had just finished it when a glance out of the window showed her that she had a visitor. It was her neighbour, Mr. Brown–HORRID HORRID HORRID Mr. Brown, as Lizzie called him. Poor man! thought Cassandra. He might be dry and dusty, but he was not horrid. Well, not very horrid!

There was a rap at the door, and John showed him in.

He was dressed in black clothes which had a smell of fustiness about them, and when he raised her hand to his lips she had to suppress a shudder, for they were as dry as old leaves.

"Miss Paxton, I can't tell you how delighted I am to see you back at home again," he said in a dry, precise voice. "I felt the sea air would not agree with you–if you remember, I

warned you against it—but I am pleased to see you have returned safely."

"You're very kind," said Cassandra, trying not to smile.

"Only honest, dear lady. As soon as I heard you had returned I knew I must call to welcome you home, and of
course, to return your book on"—he glanced at it—*"Arboreal
and Botanical Wonders."*

She thanked him for bringing it back.

"A well-stocked library is the hallmark of a great mind,"
he said.

"It's the product of many generations of my family," she
said.

"Your illustrious ancestors would be charmed to know
that it is in such good hands." His gaze fell to her hands.
"Fine hands, roughened with honest toil," he said. "Though
young, you will soon mature into a sensible woman who
will be capable of managing her husband's household to
the highest standards."

Oh, no! thought Cassandra. Surely he isn't going to propose *again*?

Her worst fears were realized as he dropped creakily to
one knee.

"Miss Paxton, will you do me the honour of becoming
my wife?"

"Mr. Brown, I have told you before—"

"Of course. Womanly modesty prevented you from

accepting my first proposal. I understand," he said, dismissing it with a wave of his hand.

"Mr. Brown," she said firmly. "I'm very sorry, but I cannot accept."

His complacent expression wavered for a moment, but then his habitual certainty returned.

"You are not yet used to being at home again. I will ask you again in a few days' time. I am sure you will see the advantages of uniting our two estates as well as our two persons—"

"Mr. Brown—"

"—the two oldest families in the area banding together for the future. Our land will stretch all the way from Farview to Millween, and our children will inherit an estate to be proud of."

"My estate is sadly mortgaged," she reminded him.

"My dear Miss Paxton, mine suffers from the same malaise. But that is all the more reason for us to marry. Once the estates are merged, we can sell off some of the outlying fields to pay the mortgages and still have an estate to be proud of," he said.

"You are very kind, but I must stand by my original answer," said Cassandra, praying for patience. "I cannot marry you."

"I will say no more for the present," he said.

Thank goodness for that, she thought.

"But I will leave you to contemplate my offer."

So saying, he bowed himself out of the room.

Well, thought Cassandra, if people aren't wanting to murder me, they are wanting to marry me! At least he had not borrowed another book, and so had no excuse to return. Although no doubt an enquiry as to whether she'd changed her mind would suffice as a reason.

She glanced at *Arboreal and Botanical Wonders* before returning it to its shelf. Perhaps if she read it, she would be able to learn something about plants—enough to stop her pulling them up by mistake, at least! But she was not in the mood for gardening, and she went upstairs instead.

As she passed the gallery, she was seized by a sudden impulse and went in. There on the walls were paintings of all her ancestors, and at the end of the row were a number of paintings of her family. There was a group portrait, showing herself, her parents, Lizzie and Rupert, and next to the group portrait there was a portrait of each of them painted individually. She traced the lines of Rupert's face. It was a handsome face, but the chin was weak and the mouth was slack. She felt a wave of sadness for her brother. She was sure he would not have trodden such a dangerous and dismal path if her parents had lived, but left to his own devices he had fallen by the wayside.

Her eyes moved on to the portrait of Lizzie. The artist had caught the curve of her lips and her golden hair very well, but had not quite captured the merriment in her eyes. The portrait of her father was better. The wide, generous mouth, the broad forehead and the hint of grey at the temples were all well caught. And then she turned to the portrait of her mother. Gentle eyes looked out at her. She missed her mother. They had always been close, and it had come as a terrible blow to learn that her mother was dead. Her eyes followed the golden hair and blue eyes and fell to the locket hanging round her neck. What had happened to her mother's locket? she wondered. She had looked for it after her mother's death, but had not been able to find it.

"Miss Cassie!" John's voice brought her thoughts back to the present. "There's mildew in the cupboard."

Cassandra gave a sigh. "Coming!" she said.

~ ~ ~

Justin was in his drawing-room of his Brighton home when Matthew was shown in.

"Mr. Standish, my lord," said Manby.

Justin looked up from the notebook he was studying.

"Interesting?" asked Matthew, nodding towards the notebook, as Manby left the room.

"Perhaps," said Justin. "I've been gathering together all our information, but so far it tells me nothing. I hope you've discovered something useful?"

Matthew sat down, lifting the tails of his coat out of the way, and then crossed one booted leg over the other.

"Nothing conclusive, but suggestive all the same. I've been asking around, and Elwin was at the races that day. He was seen by at least a dozen people."

"So he could have pushed Cassandra under the horse," said Justin thoughtfully, closing the notebook and putting it on the table beside him.

"Yes, he could, but I don't think it's likely," said Matthew. "It was a risky thing to do. He could have been seen, and besides, there was no guarantee that it would work. If she had recovered her footing she would not have fallen, and even if she had, she might not have fallen far enough forward to be in danger."

"But it was worth his while trying," said Justin. "If someone had seen him, he could have passed it off as the normal jostling that goes on at a race track, and although she might not have been killed it was a possibility. If things went well for him, he could have been rid of her with no one being any the wiser. He knew she was in Brighton, he knew she was asking about Rupert. . . . If he is the traitor's ringleader, and if he felt threatened, I think he might have felt the risk was worth his while. You've arranged for a watch to be kept on him?"

"Yes."

"Good. Because I don't want anything like this to happen

again. I want to know where he goes, what he does and who he sees. Did you discover anything else?"

"Yes, I made enquiries about Peter Raistrick, as you asked me to do."

"Yes?"

"There might be something there. He's been seen with one of the dippers. He was giving her money."

"Ah." Justin was thoughtful. "So he could have paid her to drown Cassandra?"

"He could have done. But there are . . . rumours about him."

Justin looked at him enquiringly.

Matthew raised his eyebrows and went on.

"It's rumoured that Peter likes to dress in a chemise and cap and join the women when they bathe."

Justin's lip curled. "I didn't know that."

Matthew shrugged.

"So far, they are only rumours. Several of the people I spoke to have heard he likes to do this, but not one of them has seen him actually do it. It might just be scurrilous talk. Alternatively, it might not."

"You're having him watched?" asked Justin.

"I am."

"Good. We need to know the truth of the matter, because if he really does like dressing up, he could have tried to drown Cassandra himself."

"It's certainly possible," Matthew agreed.

"Which would explain why Cassandra found it so hard to break free when she was knocked beneath the water," said Justin, following his line of thought. "A woman would have been relatively easy to fight off, but a man would have been another matter."

"Very true."

"Anything else?" asked Justin.

"Yes. I've been making enquiries about Goddard. He's in a bad way. He has a mountain of debts and no income. He tries to make his living from gambling, but he doesn't have either the luck or the skill to do it. I don't think he has the brains to be the ringleader, but if someone approached him with a difficult job and offered him enough money to do it, I think he would do anything that was asked of him."

"Then he could be our man. Do we know where he was when Cassandra was bathing?"

"He was supposedly out of town, but I'm making enquiries to see if that is true."

"Good. Are all the men being watched?"

"Yes. They are."

"I want this finished with as quickly as possible," said Justin, standing up.

"I'm not surprised," said Matthew.

Justin looked at him enquiringly.

"As soon as it's finished, Cassandra can come back to Brighton," said Matthew.

"Meaning?"

"Meaning that you've been like a bear with a sore head whilst she's been away. You miss her."

Justin acknowledged the truth of it.

"Yes, I do."

~　~　~

Cassandra could not sleep. It was now five days since she had left Brighton and she had still heard nothing from Justin. She did not know how things were progressing in Brighton, or if they were progressing at all. She turned over and plumped her pillow, then closed her eyes and counted sheep. Unfortunately, the shepherd began to look remarkably like Justin. He was walking towards her, stroking her face, kissing her—

She sat up resolutely. If she allowed herself to think of Justin, she would never fall asleep. She decided to get up and choose a book to read. Inspiration hit. She would read *Arboreal and Botanical Wonders*. That should keep her thoughts from straying to anything romantic! It should also help her with the flower-beds when she plucked up the courage to weed them.

Throwing a wrapper round her shoulders she lit her candle with a tinderbox and then, picking it up, she went downstairs. The library looked serene in the moonlight, which came in through the french window. She put her candle down on the table and went over to the first shelf, looking along it until she found what she sought. She picked it up, collected her candle, and went out into the hall. As she did so, she heard a tinkling sound, as of glass breaking, and immediately she stiffened. She turned her head towards the dining-room, which was where the sound had come from. She strained her ears, but could hear nothing. And then she heard a creak, and knew at once what it was: the creaking floorboard in the middle of the dining-room floor. Someone had broken into the house, a burglar or . . .

She did not dare follow that thought. Hurrying upstairs, she ran into her bedroom with her heart pounding. She threw her book down on a chair and locked the door, pressing against it and listening hard, trying to catch any sound that would tell her where the burglar was.

It must be a burglar, she told herself. It couldn't be someone who had followed her from Brighton. No one knew she was going, except Maria, and Maria had not wanted to tell anyone.

But someone could have seen her leave. . . .

She caught the sound of a groan, and recognized it as the groan of one of the stairs halfway up the staircase. She held her breath. There came another groan, more like a whine this time: it was the second stair from the top. Seeing the candle, she quickly blew out the flame so that no light would show under her door, then she listened again. There was nothing. She waited. And waited. And . . . the door handle began to turn. She felt her heart thudding in her chest. There was someone on the other side of the door. They tried to open it, but the lock held. They put their shoulder against it, but the door was made of oak and the lock was a strong one, and did not give.

But now they knew she was in there. Or rather, they knew that someone was in there. What would they do next? She glanced at the window, but was reassured. It was inaccessible. There were no trees nearby, and no creepers on the walls. Without a ladder, it would be impossible to climb in, and her ladder was broken. Unless the burglar had brought a ladder with him.

She heard a slight creak and let out a sigh of relief, knowing they had moved away from the door. But where had they gone? She fought down an impulse to open the door and look. She knew she had to stay locked in her room until morning. She could only hope that John would be safe. But if the intruder was a burglar, he was unlikely to want to harm anyone, and if he was an assassin, sent to kill her, he would have no reason to harm her servant.

She stayed by the door until she was sure the intruder would not come back, then padded over to the bed. All hope of sleep was gone. So, too, was all hope of reading.

The curtains were pulled across the window, and there was no moonlight coming in from outside. She did not intend to pull them back, and she did not want to risk lighting a candle. Instead, she huddled under the covers and waited for daylight.

At last it came, creeping through a crack in the curtain. She felt drowsy, and realized she must have dozed off. But she was still safe, and in one piece. She waited until it was fully light before getting out of bed and cautiously peering round the curtain. The lawns lay peaceful and serene beneath another fine sky. There was no sign of any disturbance.

She washed quickly, using water left over from her ablutions the previous evening, and then dressed. She hesitated before unlocking the door, only turning the key when she heard John's heavy tread outside and knew that he was up. She dressed and went downstairs quickly.

"We'll have breakfast in the kitchen," she said, as she joined him.

She did not feel equal to examining the damage from the night before until she had eaten.

"Just as you say, miss."

She prepared breakfast whilst John saw to the horses, never thinking it odd that she was waiting on her servant, for whenever the occasion demanded she helped with the chores. A short while later, having breakfasted, she went into the dining-room, and there, sure enough, was a broken window. She looked around to see if anything else had been taken or disturbed, but apart from the window, everything looked exactly as it should be.

"We seem to have had a break in," she said, as she met John in the hall. "The dining-room window is smashed."

"It's a wonder we weren't murdered in our beds," said John.

Cassandra shivered.

"It'll be Ned Rogers," said John. "He's as shifty as they come."

"It could be," said Cassandra cautiously, thinking of the local ne'er-do-well. "I will have to tell Sir William. As the local magistrate, he will need to know."

"I'll go and tell him," said John.

"Good," said Cassandra. "I want to have it dealt with before we return to Brighton."

She had not been intending to return until the traitors' ringleader had been caught, but she no longer felt safe on her estate. It could have been a simple burglary, but she felt sure there was more to it. If it had been a burglary, then something would have been taken. She felt sure in her own mind that someone from Brighton had discovered her where-abouts. In the country, she was more vulnerable than in the town. Her house was large and there were many windows, any one of which could be broken, whereas in Brighton the house was much smaller and she would have Justin's help. He would arrange for someone to watch the house, and she would feel safer that way.

There was a rap at the door, and Cassandra jumped. Before she could stop him, John opened the door and Mr. Brown walked in.

"I hope I don't intrude?" he said, smiling.

"No, come in," said Cassandra with a flood of relief. She had never been so glad to see Mr. Brown in her life!

"You might as well. Everyone else does," said John. "There's been a burglary."

"No?"

"Yes. Broken glass all over the carpet."

"The same thing happened to me last week. Something ought to be done about it," he said, tut tutting as he shook his head.

"You had a break in?" asked Cassandra.

"Yes. On Tuesday. The window in the pantry was broken. Mrs. Deeling was very upset."

Cassandra felt hope stirring. It seemed as though the break in might have been nothing more than a common burglary after all—although nothing had been taken, she reminded herself. But perhaps the burglar had not expected to find her at home. Then, hearing her going upstairs, he had tried the bedroom door and, finding it locked, he decided the house was occupied and that he had better leave.

"I am going to alert Sir William," she said.

"My dear Miss Paxton, you mustn't trouble your head over such a matter. I will tell him myself. I am going to see him this morning to find out if he has made any progress on my affair."

She was pleased to accept Mr. Brown's offer. It would allow her to go back to Brighton all the sooner, for although the break in might have been nothing serious, she preferred to take no chances.

"Thank you, that's very kind."

"A gentleman is useful on these occasions," said Mr. Brown significantly. "It is hard for a young lady to deal with these matters. But I will say no more at present. Perhaps next week . . ."

"I won't be here next week," said Cassandra. "I am returning to Brighton."

"So soon?" he asked.

"Yes. I came home only to bring some furniture."

"I had hoped you would stay longer, but I must not deprive you of your pleasure," he said meticulously.

"If you will excuse me, I must get ready to leave," she said.

Mr. Brown looked as though he would like to detain her and then changed his mind.

"Of course," he said.

And bowing low over her hand he left.

"I want you to have the coach ready for this afternoon," she said to John.

"Very good, miss"

Cassandra looked round. The house had seemed so peaceful when she had returned, a haven of safety and tranquillity. But now a cloud had been cast over it and she would be glad to be away.

John began to walk towards the door. Before he could go out, however, she stopped him.

"Do you remember last year," she asked, "when Mr. Rupert brought a print home? It had a picture of France on it, and a picture of the English coast, too. There were balloons flying over it, and rowing boats going across it."

"And a tunnel going under the sea," said John with a rumble of laughter.

"Yes, that's the one. Do you remember who gave it to Mr. Rupert?"

John thought. "Wait a minute. It's on the tip of my tongue. It was like my father's name. Edwin he was called, but it wasn't Edwin. It was something like it, though. . . ."

"Elwin," said Cassandra, with a sinking feeling.

John gave a satisfied smile.

"That was it," he said. "Mr. Elwin."

CHAPTER TEN

It was early evening by the time the coach rolled into Brighton once more. Cassandra instructed John to stop at Justin's house on the Steyne.

"You must come inside with me," said Cassandra, as he opened the door and let down the step. "I can't go in alone."

"I should think not, Miss Cassie," said John, horrified at the mere thought of it.

He closed the door behind her and the two of them approached Justin's house.

Cassandra rapped on the door. A moment later Manby appeared, looking as haughty as ever. When he saw her, he relented slightly.

"Yes, miss?" he said.

"I am here to see Lord Deverill."

"I'm sorry, miss, but Lord Deverill is not at home."

"Not at home?"

This was a blow.

"No, miss He has gone out for the evening."

"Do you know what time he will be back?" she asked.

"No, miss, I'm afraid I don't."

"In that case, would you give him a message for me?"

"Of course, miss"

"Would you ask him to call on me at his earliest convenience?"

"Yes, miss. I'll give him the message as soon as he returns."

Cassandra climbed into the coach and was once more on her way, traversing the streets until she reached her own front door. So much had happened since she had left it just under a week before that she felt she had been away for a month. She only wished her return could have been under happier circumstances, for she had not meant to come back until matters had been resolved. But it could not be helped. Events had forced her hand.

She unlocked the door and went into the house, locking it again behind her. There were no candles lit in the hall and it was dark.

"Moll!" she called.

She heard the sound of Moll coming upstairs from the

kitchen. The candle bobbed into view, with Moll's surprised face behind it.

"Miss Cassie? Is that you? I wasn't expecting you back today. 'It's too late,' I told myself. 'She won't be home to-day.'"

"It isn't so very late," said Cassandra, removing her bonnet and putting it down on a console table.

"You look pinched," said Moll. "Have you been sitting in a draught?"

"No," said Cassandra.

"That coach needs its windows looking at," fussed Moll. "I'll light the fire. It's come colder this evening."

"No, there's no need for a fire," said Cassandra. "I'm not cold. I am just a little worried, that's all."

"Worried?"

Moll pulled a fierce face, as if to say that anyone who had worried her mistress had best look to their safety.

"We had a break in on the estate," explained Cassandra. "It has made me anxious. Are all the doors locked here?"

"That they are. There's some lawless bodies in Brighton," said Moll, as though it was a renowned den of iniquity.

"And the windows?" asked Cassandra.

"They're all closed, Miss Cassie, and if you're worried, they'll stay closed."

The weather had become cooler, and there was no need for them to be open.

"Good," said Cassandra. "I expect I am worrying unnecessarily, but for the next week, at least, I would like to be careful."

"I've said so all along," declared Moll darkly. "It's a wonder we haven't all been murdered in our beds long since."

Cassandra was relieved that, without telling Moll the real cause of her concerns, she had been able to make sure the house was secure. With Justin away, and with her guards believing she was in the country, she would not be watched, so she must make sure she protected herself.

"I will just wash the grime of travelling away, and then I would like a cup of tea."

Half an hour later Cassandra was sitting in the parlour, dressed in a fresh gown. Barely had she settled herself on the sofa when there came a rap at the door.

"That will be Lord Deverill," said Cassandra. "John has taken the coach round to the coach house. I'll answer the door."

"You will not, Miss Cassie. If you've a mind to see him this time, I'll let him in."

Moll left the room, and a few moments later announced, "Lord Deverill."

Justin strode into the room. His coat was creased and his breeches rumpled, whilst his boots were covered in mud. He looked as though he had been riding hard. His hair was unkempt, and fell in dishevelled locks around his face.

"The tea, please, Moll," said Cassandra.

"Tea?" asked Moll suspiciously, as though scenting a ruse to remove her from the room.

"Yes, please," said Cassandra firmly. "Bring two cups, and the tea."

Grumbling under her breath, Moll left the room.

"I came as soon as I got your message," said Justin, once Moll had closed the door. He strode over to Cassandra's side.

"Won't you sit down?" she said.

He sat on the sofa, and she sat down opposite him.

"My boots . . ." he said, belatedly realizing they were covered in mud.

"It doesn't matter," said Cassandra. "I need to speak to you."

"You shouldn't have come back to Brighton. We agreed that you would not return until I had captured the leader of the traitors. It isn't safe for you to be here. You could be subjected to another so-called accident."

"I had no choice. I had to come back," she said, twisting her hands in her lap. "There was a break in. . . ." she began.

She had his full attention as she told him exactly what had happened to her on her estate.

"This is bad," he said, shaking his head. "This is very bad." He frowned. "Someone must have known you were going home."

"Unless the burglary was unrelated. My neighbour had a burglary only last week."

He pursed his lips.

"It's possible, but I think we must assume it was connected until we are sure. I will have someone watching over you night and day. But it will be safer if you stay indoors. I can provide you with some new servants, a butler and two footmen. They will be my own men, and they will know how to deal with any dangerous situations that might arise. I will have the house watched as well."

"Thank you, but I cannot stay indoors for ever. I prefer to carry on with my life, though I have no objection to taking a footman with me when I go out. He can protect me should the need arise."

Justin looked unhappy with the arrangement, but did not object.

"Very well," he said. "Did anyone know?" he went on. "Did you tell anyone you were going away?" he asked.

"Only Maria," she said.

He stood up.

"Which means that everyone else in Brighton would have known within a few hours."

"No," Cassandra said. "I know Maria likes to gossip but she didn't tell anyone, I'm sure of it. She didn't want to tell anyone, and she didn't want me to tell anyone. She thought that if people knew I was moving furniture with a view to selling my town house, news of my poverty would spread, and she does not want people to know that I am in difficult circumstances. So you see, Maria would not have told anyone. Besides, there is something else."

He looked at her enquiringly.

"It occurred to me that John might remember who had given Rupert the print. Rupert was very fond of him, and I thought they might have talked about it. So I asked John if Rupert had told him."

"And?"

"It was Mr. Elwin."

"Elwin." Justin nodded, then sat down again, leaning his elbows on his knees. "Yes, that makes sense."

"Is he the ringleader, do you think?" asked Cassandra.

"It's possible. He has the brains for it, and also the ruthlessness. We've had our eye on him for some time, but we have no evidence against him."

"Then I suggest we find some," said Cassandra.

He looked at her enquiringly.

"I am tired to waiting for someone to attack me," she said. "I can't sit cowering in my house for ever. I want to tempt the would-be assassin to come into the open. I think we should encourage him to strike."

He frowned.

"Do you mean you are offering yourself as bait?"

"Yes, I am."

"No." He shook his head. "It's too dangerous."

"I cannot live in fear for ever. I would rather try and trap the killer. And once we catch him, you will have some evidence against him. Not of treachery, it's true, but of a crime. Then you can turn him over to the authorities."

He gave a heavy sigh and sat down, then said reluctantly, "There's something in what you say."

"There is. Tempting him is no more dangerous than waiting for him to strike. Probably less so, as he will strike at a time and place of our choosing."

He nodded. "Very well. I agree. It seems our man is Elwin. I will find out where he is going for the next week. If he is going to any public functions it will be possible for you to go there, too."

"And if he has hired someone to kill me, instead of doing it himself?"

"Then we will catch them and make them talk," he said. "We only need them to confirm that they are in Elwin's pay, and we have him."

The door opened and Moll entered the room, carrying a large tray.

"I've brung the tea," she said, glowering first at Cassandra and then at Justin.

He sat back in his chair, creating a distance between himself and Cassandra.

"Thank you, Moll," said Cassandra. "That will be all,"

she said, as Moll placed the tray on a console table and then lingered.

"Good. Then I can get on with my mending," said Moll, walking over to the side of the room where she had left a basket of mending. She sat down on a hard-backed chair and took a sheet out of the basket.

Cassandra glowered at her but she took no notice.

"My sister's ball is in a few days' time," said Justin, glancing at Moll and then back at Cassandra. "I will let you know all the news when I see you there."

Cassandra nodded. She poured the tea.

"In the meantime," he said, taking the cup she handed to him and drinking the tea in one go, "it would be better if you stay indoors."

He put his cup down.

"I agree," said Cassandra. Glancing at Moll, who was looking at her curiously, she added, "The weather has been inclement, and I have plenty to do in the house."

He stood up.

"Until the ball, then."

"Until the ball."

He looked as though he would like to say something further, but after hesitating for a moment he made her a bow. Moll laid aside her mending and showed him out.

"A fine gennulmen," said Moll, when she returned to the room. She looked at Cassandra significantly. "A very fine gennulman. Too fine to be coming here at all hours for no reason."

Cassandra did not want to answer the questions she saw hovering on Moll's lips and turned away. Just when she thought she had resolved her feelings for Justin, they had become confused all over again. She had settled her feelings concerning her brother's death, and although they still cast a shadow over her from time to time she had forgiven Justin his part in it. But she had never thought she would do more than that. Yet here she was, turning to him without hesitation when she found herself in danger, and putting her trust in him. Moreover, she had enjoyed seeing him again, and felt the loss of him now that he had gone.

Putting the disturbing thoughts from her mind she said, "I will have supper now, Moll, please."

To her relief, Moll said no more about Justin, and contented herself with replying, "Very good, miss"

CHAPTER ELEVEN

Cassandra found herself looking forward to Anne's ball. She had spent the time since her return from her estate in cleaning the remaining rooms, beating the rugs and polishing the furniture, so that now the house was ready for sale. As soon as the ball was over, she meant to speak to her lawyer and make the necessary arrangements. It was good to have the ball to look forward to, a cheerful event to offset the gloom of parting with her house.

She had no new gowns to wear, having worn every respectable dress she possessed, and so she had accepted Maria's loan of a dress. The two of them were almost the same size, and although Cassandra was the taller of the two, the dress had swept the floor on Maria so that, as Cassandra looked in the cheval glass on the evening of the ball, she was pleased to see that it still reached the ground on her. It was made of pink silk, with a pretty trim of roses round the high waist, and a cluster of roses on the short, puffed sleeve. To match the trim, she had put a simple wreath of fresh roses in her hair.

Maria called for her promptly in the carriage and together Cassandra, Maria and Harry set out for Granmere Park. Maria gossiped comfortably all the way there, telling Cassandra of everything she had done since they had last seen each other, and Cassandra told Maria most of what she had been doing, so that the journey passed quickly and they soon found themselves at their destination.

The house was ablaze with light as they approached, forming a bright spot in the gloom. Rain was falling steadily from the already darkening sky and Maria's coachman held an umbrella over the ladies as they descended from the carriage and went into the house. Harry followed them, cursing the weather.

Once inside, they found that they were not the first to arrive. There were already a large number of guests there, filling the magnificent hall with light and colour. The young ladies' white muslins blended with the older ladies' coloured silks; lace fans mixed with ostrich feathers; diamonds mixed with pearls; and all were set off by the marble columns and the splendid marble floor. The sound of violins drifted out from the ballroom, mixing with the lively chatter in the hall.

Cassandra, Maria and Harry proceeded to the foot of the stairs where they were welcomed by Anne and her husband, Charles. Charles was a solid young man some five years older than Anne, with a good-natured air. After being welcomed, Cassandra, Maria and Harry went into the ballroom. It was a spacious room, and looked quite different to the last time they had seen it. Then, it had been an empty space, with high ceilings and large windows letting in the daylight. Now, it was full of life and colour, and was lit by hundreds of candles. A set of dancers were enjoying the cotillion, whilst other guests stood around the side of the room and talked.

There were a number of people Cassandra recognized, and after nodding to her various acquaintances she found that her hand was sought by Mr. Kingsley. He was dressed in even greater style this evening. His coat was so tight he could barely move his arms, and his waistcoat glittered with gold thread. His stockings showed off a fine calf, and his black pumps adorned his dainty feet. As he led her out on to the floor, she glanced instinctively at his wrist. No, there was no mole. Laughing at herself for suspecting him—how could he have tried to drown her, when men and women bathed separately?—she allowed her gaze to wander over the room. She could not see Justin, and wondered if he had arrived.

". . . run of bad luck," Mr. Kingsley was saying, when she returned her attention to him. "Went to the races again and lost again. Thought m'horse would do it. Good form. But came in last. Commiserated with Goddard. His run of luck's been worse than mine. Takes it like a man. Don't complain. Laughs it off. That's the spirit. Don't know where he gets the blunt from. Doesn't work. Father a pauper. Lives on tick. But he seems to manage. Joined him in the refreshment tent. Queer cove. Doesn't care a button for his clothes. Doesn't know a mailcoach from a waterfall."

Fortunately, Cassandra knew he was referring to styles of cravats, and made a suitably astonished exclamation.

"Knew you'd be shocked," said Mr. Kingsley seriously.

By the time the dance came to an end, there was still no sign of Justin. Cassandra danced with an officer, resplendent in his scarlet coat, and her hand was then solicited by Lord Armington.

"Will you give me the honour of this dance?" he asked.

"I'd be delighted," she replied.

As she took his hand, she glanced at his wrist. There was no mole.

I'm becoming suspicious of everyone, she thought with an inward sigh. But in the circumstances, she felt it was better to be suspicious of everyone, no matter how innocent they seemed, rather than find herself in danger again.

"I have not seen you recently," he said, as the dance began. "I looked for you at the assembly rooms last week, but you were not there."

"No," she said, without revealing where she had been.

"A pity. You will be going next week?"

"I don't know," she replied. "My plans are not fixed."

"I see."

He turned the conversation to the recent change in the weather, and from there to the theatre and the shops. Cassandra joined in, but she found the conversation something of a strain and was glad when the dance was over. She wanted to speak to Justin, and everything else seemed unimportant.

She was about to rejoin Maria and Harry when she saw the Kerriths at the far side of the room. As she watched the beautiful Miss Kerrith flirting with her fan, Cassandra had a sudden flash of memory. The lace on the fan reminded her of the lace used to trim Miss Kerrith's bathing cap. The young beauty had been swimming at the same time as Cassandra. What if she had been the one to push her under the water?

Cassandra had been convinced that the attempts on her life had had something to do with her brother, but what if that was not the case? What if they had been made for a different reason? Miss Kerrith had seen Justin taking her into supper at the assembly rooms. What if she had sensed a rival, and decided to put her out of the way? It seemed absurd, and yet Miss Kerrith had also been at the races. . . .

Overcome with curiosity, Cassandra moved nearer Miss Kerrith. Had the heiress a mole? It was impossible to tell. She was wearing long white evening gloves. But if she went to the ladies' withdrawing room at any time during the evening she might take them off.

Cassandra found her attention claimed by a jovial old man who had known her father and she enjoyed reminiscing with him. Afterwards, she talked to a dowager she had met in the library. But all the time she watched Miss Kerrith, and followed her from the room when that young lady withdrew.

It was cool in the corridor. Cassandra followed Miss Kerrith to a small room that had been set aside for the use of the ladies. A number of maids were there, waiting for their mistresses in case they needed anything. Some were already ministering to their mistresses, mending torn hems or passing them fresh handkerchiefs.

Miss Kerrith called imperiously to her maid and commanded the girl to dab her temples with lavender water, berating her for using too much on one temple and not enough on the other. Then she stripped off her evening gloves and, snatching the lavender water from her maid, dabbed some of it on her own wrists.

Seizing her chance, Cassandra crossed the room.

"What a beautiful scent," she said, taking Miss Kerrith's hand before she could protest. "It really is quite lovely."

Under pretence of smelling the lavender, Cassandra

examined Miss Kerrith's wrists, only to feel foolish as again she saw there was no mole. Miss Kerrith looked astonished at Cassandra's behaviour, but soon melted before the flattery, and revealed that the scent had been specially made for her to a secret family recipe.

Cassandra congratulated her on her taste, then made her excuses and left the withdrawing room. So Miss Kerrith had not tried to drown her. But as she returned to the ballroom, Cassandra realized she had not been able to examine the wrists of Miss Kerrith's mother.

Hardly had she taken her place at the side of the room when she felt a presence at her shoulder, and turned round to see Justin standing there. He was immaculately dressed in tailcoat and knee breeches, and his dark hair had been brushed into a fashionable style. He smiled down at her and her heart missed a beat.

"Might I have this dance?" he asked.

"Of course," she said, knowing that the dance would offer them an opportunity of talking without attracting the attention of the gossip mongers.

"I have found out Elwin's plans for the next two weeks," he said, as the music began.

"How did you manage it?" she asked.

"His valet is dissatisfied. Elwin is a difficult master, and pays poorly. He should know better. Disgruntled servants are always eager to talk."

"Is he going anywhere I can go, too?" asked Cassandra.

"Yes. He's going to the Pavilion next week."

"The Pavilion?" she asked in surprise.

The steps of the dance parted them, but when they came together again, he said, "Yes. The Pavilion. The Prince of Wales has a range of friends drawn from all walks of life. Some are from the nobility, but others, like Elwin, are from the lower orders. They are good company, being witty and charming. As long as a man can amuse him, the Prince is satisfied. He cares for nothing else. Let a man once bore him, and that man will never be invited to the Pavilion again."

"But I cannot go there," said Cassandra, disappointed.

"Yes, you can. I have an invitation for the same night as Elwin. I can arrange for you to be there as well."

"How?" she asked.

"The Prince is always willing to invite beautiful young ladies to his parties," he remarked.

"Would Maria be able to come, too?"

"Sadly not. But the Prince likes my sister and he will be willing for me to take her with me. I know she will be happy to chaperon you. She has never been to the Pavilion, and has always wanted to go. She wants to see if the Prince's chimney piece is as splendid as her own!"

Cassandra smiled, then became serious again. "Then it seems that that is what we must do. But do you really think the murderer would strike at the Pavilion?" she asked. "It doesn't seem the kind of place to suit an accident."

"On the contrary, nothing would be easier than to stage an accident at the door. There is always a crush of carriages at the start and end of the evening, and a swift push could send you beneath one. It would seem like nothing but a regrettable accident, and in all the confusion and excitement of arrival, no one would see that you had been pushed."

Cassandra shivered. The idea seemed suddenly dangerous. What if the murderer managed to do what they wanted to do? A quick push, a rearing horse, a carriage wheel . . .

"We don't have to go any further if you don't want to," said Justin, as if reading her thoughts. "In fact, the more I think about it, the more I don't like the idea. It's too great a risk. We will abandon the plan."

"No," said Cassandra. "It is a risk, it's true, but I must bring this to an end. I will be returning to my estate next week. Lizzie will be coming home, and I don't want her put in danger if the murderer is still loose. I want to have the matter finished with as quickly as possible."

"Very well. There will be a lot of men there to protect you, dressed as coachmen and footmen. Some of the guests will be there to protect you, too. I will be there, although I will not be with you. If we are to tempt the villain to strike, then we must make him think you are not being watched."

She nodded.

"I hope he strikes at the start of the evening, rather than at the end," she said lightly. "Then I'll be able to enjoy my evening at the Pavilion. I've always wanted to see it."

"It's certainly a place to be seen," said Justin.

"Rupert was invited once," she said, determined to turn the conversation on to lighter ground. "He said it was full of dragons. He didn't mean live ones, I hope?"

"No," he said with a smile. "But you will see plenty of them, all the same. They are on the wallpaper and coiled round pillars. They are one of the Prince's favourite motifs."

She warmed to the conversation. Despite the danger, she was looking forward to seeing the Prince's home.

"I've heard a lot about the Pavilion. Is it as exotic as it sounds?" she asked, as the dance came to an end.

"It's like walking into a dream," said Justin, as he walked her from the floor. "The Prince has too much time on his hands and not enough to do. He seems to spend most of his time these days remodelling the Pavilion. Goodness knows what it will look like when it is finished. Like something out of the Arabian Nights, I suspect."

"It will be something to tell Lizzie about," said Cassandra.

As long as Mr. Elwin doesn't succeed with his plan, she thought. But she did not say it out loud. She told herself that she was in no danger. Justin would be there, as well as a large number of other people, all making sure she was protected. And she, too, would be on her guard. Knowing when danger was likely to strike, and in what way, she was armed against it. She might lose her footing if she was pushed, but she would not be taken by surprise and she would be able to regain it. Or so she hoped. She concentrated instead on thinking of the treat in store. Not many people were invited to the Pavilion, and she meant to make the most of it.

~ ~ ~

The next morning brought another letter from Lizzie. Cassandra was glad of it. She found it hard to settle to anything, knowing that soon she would be offering herself up as a murderer's bait. But her sister's light-hearted epistle was just what she needed. She took the letter from Moll, who had brought it into the parlour.

"Sit down, Moll," she said, "and we'll see what she has to say."

Moll needed no second bidding. She settled herself on a chair by the fireplace, directly opposite Cassandra, and listened with rapt attention as Cassandra began.

Darling, darling Cassie,
Thank you so much for saying Jane can come and stay.

Moll looked at Cassandra enquiringly.

"In her last letter, Lizzie asked me if Jane could stay. I read it in the country," she explained.

Moll nodded, satisfied, and Cassandra continued with the letter.

She is in your det FOREVER. We have been to the library and have borrowed a book by Mrs. Radcliffe which is quite HORRID....

"Horrid seems to be her favourite word at the moment," said Cassandra, breaking off.

"Aah," said Moll sagely.

Cassandra began to read again.

... It is all about a heroin who gets married and has a misterious husband and Jane and I are NEVER getting married unless we meet a markwiss, and Jane says she would prefer a dook. But I am going to marry a markwiss with a scar across his cheek because he has been in a duel fighting for the honour of the lady he loves ...

"I wonder who that might be?" asked Cassandra with a laugh.

"It'll be Miss Lizzie," said Moll seriously. "A nice marquess would be just the thing."

I'd be at a ball and I'd have a ostrich fether fan. I'd waft it in front of me and say, Thank you, my lord, you may tempt me

to a glass of shampain, and How kind of you, Your Grace. A
dish of oysters would be most welcum. Then I'd see him—my
markwiss—and he'd see me and say to his friend "Who is that
bewty? The one with the gowlden hair? Introduce me." He'd
ask me to dance, and then he'd ask me to marry him.

"Ahh," said Moll again, entranced by Lizzie's picture.
"That's how it'll be."

"She might not marry a marquess," Cassandra pointed
out reasonably.

"No," said Moll, roused to battle on behalf of her be-
loved Lizzie, "she might marry a prince instead," and she
glared at Cassandra, as though daring her to contradict
her.

Cassandra did not dare, but instead folded the letter and
put it away.

"That might be Lizzie's prince now," said Cassandra
humorously as there came a rap at the door.

"Hrumph!" said Moll, standing up. "John's gone to see
to the horses. I'd best see who that is."

It will be Justin, thought Cassandra, tidying her hair in
front of the mirror, but when the drawing-room door opened
it was not Justin who was shown in, it was Lord Armington.

"Lord Armington," said Cassandra in surprise.

"Miss Paxton. I am glad to find you at home."

"It is good of you to call. Won't you sit down?"

"Thank you, but I prefer to stand."

Cassandra had a sudden presentiment of what was to come. She knew that any young lady would be glad to receive an offer from Lord Armington, with his dark good looks, his elegant dress, and his air of good breeding, but if he asked for her hand, she knew she must turn him down.

"I am glad I have found you at home as I have something particular to say to you," said Lord Armington. "You must know how I esteem and admire you. From the first moment I saw you in the Assembly Rooms I was struck with your face, and the time I have spent in your company since has taught me that your breeding and character match your beauty." He knelt elegantly before her. "Miss Paxton, will you be so good as to bestow upon me your hand in marriage?"

"Lord Armington, do, please get up," said Cassandra. "I am very sorry . . . it is such an honour . . . I am conscious of the very great favour you have done me in asking me to be your wife . . . but I'm afraid I can't accept."

"Not accept?"

His tone of voice, and his expression, betrayed his surprise. And small wonder, thought Cassandra with an inward sigh. A man of his worth must never have imagined that his suit would be rejected.

"I'm afraid not."

He behaved with dignity and decorum, standing up and dusting an imaginary speck of dirt from his knees, as though kneeling on the floor and then rising again was the most ordinary occupation.

"May I ask why not?" he asked.

"I'm afraid I don't love you," she said.

"Ah." He became thoughtful. Then he said, "I believe this is your first summer of engagements?"

"Yes, it is, but that has nothing to do with the matter, I assure you."

"Perhaps, perhaps not. Only time will tell. You will allow me to say that it is not unusual for young ladies to look for love when they first come out. I know that your entry into society has been delayed because of the sad circumstances surrounding your family in recent years, and I understand that you have seen little yet of life. Perhaps when you have had a chance to do so you will feel differently. My own feelings will not change. I cannot profess a deep and abiding passion, but having outgrown my youth I am pleased rather than otherwise, as passion can be very uncomfortable. But I have an eye for beauty, and you are the most exquisite young lady I have ever seen. It is no idle compliment," he said, when she tried to protest. "I am something of a connoisseur, and I can tell you that your beauty has no equal. I would still like to be able to call you my wife. At the moment the charms of a comfortable, I may even say luxurious, establishment, do not weigh heavily with you, but in the future, perhaps, they might. I should also mention that your sister would be most welcome. There is plenty of room for her at Armington House. She would have all the best masters, in addition to her seminary, and I would regard it as my duty—indeed my pleasure—to help you arrange her come out, and to give her a marriage portion, so that she might be well settled in life."

"Thank you, you are most kind," said Cassandra, feeling more and more sorry that she could not accept him.

He smiled at her.

"I honour you for your feelings," he said. "If you contract a love match I will wish you happy. But if you do not, you have only to say a word to have my offer renewed. Until then, Miss Paxton, I will bid you good day."

He made her a low bow and withdrew.

Cassandra clasped her hands in front of her and walked over to the fireplace. She stopped short as she caught sight of her face in the gilded mirror hanging above it. She looked worried. And small wonder. She had just turned down a most eligible offer, one that would have ensured her future comfort, and Lizzie's future prosperity as well.

Have I been foolish? were the words etched across her face. She did not want luxury for herself, but she did not just have herself to think of. She had Lizzie, too. She could provide for them both after a fashion, but was that enough?

The little girl might be happy now, when all she needed was a pony, but as she grew older she would have different needs. Fashionable clothes, a season, a chance to marry . . . and Cassandra would not be able to give her them. But Lord Armington would, and he had made it clear that he would do it gladly. To offer Lizzie a marriage portion . . . it was extraordinarily kind.

She heard footsteps in the hall. Pinching her cheeks to put a little colour into them, she turned and faced the door. It was opened to reveal Maria.

"Cassie! I've just seen Lord Armington leaving your house," said Maria, her eyes shining with excitement. "Don't keep me in suspense. Has he proposed?"

Cassandra gave a rueful smile. "Yes."

"Oh, Cassie, congratulations! I knew how it would be. I have said so all along. You will be Lady Armington! You will have clothes and carriages and a house in town. Lady Armington! How well it sounds. I can only hope you won't be too grand to speak to me when you are married."

Cassandra could bear no more.

"Maria, I turned him down."

Maria looked stunned.

"You turned him down?" she gasped.

"Yes."

"But Cassie, why? Everything that is most eligible . . . An offer like that will not come again."

"I know."

Maria shook her head. "I don't understand you," she said.

"I couldn't marry him because I don't love him," said Cassandra simply.

"There is more to marriage than love," said Maria.

"That is easy for you to say, but would you have married Harry if you hadn't loved him?" asked Cassandra.

"No," Maria admitted, "but that's different. I didn't have a mortgaged estate and a sister to care for. And besides, I can't see why you don't love Lord Armington. I'm sure it can't be difficult. He's handsome, charming and well mannered. He's interesting, and he sincerely values you, and he would welcome Lizzie."

"Yes, I know he would, he told me so himself. But I just couldn't do it."

Maria looked downcast.

"Oh, Cassie, I was hoping you'd make a good marriage so that you would be able to keep your town house," she said. "Without it you will hardly ever be in Brighton. You can stay with us at any time, you know that, but it is not the same. We will miss you."

"You will have to come and stay with us in the country."

"Of course we will, but I did so want to have you here. Oh, well, never mind," said Maria, putting her gloom behind her. "At least we have you for another week or so. We will have to make the most of it. We will be giving a small dinner party on Wednesday. Perhaps you might like one of the gentlemen there."

"I am beginning to agree with Harry. You are incorrigible!" said Cassandra.

"But you will come to my party all the same," said Maria.

"I'm afraid I can't," said Cassandra. "I would like to, but I am going to the Pavilion."

Maria was momentarily speechless.

"The *Pavilion*?" she said at last.

"Yes."

"To see *the Prince of Wales*?"

"I believe he lives there, yes," Cassandra teased her.

"Well! I never thought . . . I never imagined . . . Cassie, this is wonderful. I am green with envy. Who are you going with? How did you secure an invitation?"

"I am going with Lord Deverill's sister," she said.

"Lord Deverill's sister," said Maria, casting her a thoughtful glance.

"Yes. It is just kindness," said Cassandra, trying to fend off the questions she could see hovering on Maria's lips.

"Of course," said Maria with a straight face. "She invites all her casual acquaintances to go to the Pavilion. Will her brother be there?" she added nonchalantly.

"I believe so," said Cassandra.

Maria's eyes sparkled.

"Now I know why you turned down Lord Armington."

"Maria, you're wrong."

"You can't lie to me. I know there has been something between you and Lord Deverill recently but I didn't like to say anything because I believed it was causing you pain, but there is something about you when you are with him. You seem more alive than when he is not there. I think you are meant to be together," she said simply.

"There is nothing in the acquaintance, I assure you," said Cassandra.

"Very well, if you say so, then I will pretend to believe you."

Cassandra felt uncomfortable, and was glad when Maria changed the subject.

"Have you decided what you will wear?" Maria asked.

"No. I don't have anything suitable," said Cassandra.

"Neither do I, or you would be welcome to borrow it," said Maria. "You must have something new."

"It's impossible," said Cassandra with a sigh.

"You can't meet the Prince of Wales in an old frock," said Maria.

Cassandra hesitated. What Maria said was very true.

"Cassie, you must have something new. If you are determined to sell the town house, then some of the proceeds will pay for it. Madame Joubier will not mind waiting a few months for payment, and if she knows you are going to the Pavilion she will give you a favourable price. If one of her creations is seen in such exclusive company, it will be bound to bring more business in her way."

Cassandra was tempted.

"Perhaps I might have something new," she said hesitantly.

Maria stood up.

"I am going to take you to her salon right away, before you change your mind."

"She won't see me without an appointment," Cassandra prevaricated.

"When she knows you are going to dine with the Prince, she will see you straight away," said Maria.

"And she won't be able to have anything ready so quickly."

"She always keeps a few gowns half made for emergencies. She told me so when I visited her once, in need of a new gown in a hurry. I was delighted to find she had a good selection that were partially made up, ready for just such an event. She will dress you for the Pavilion if she has to keep a team of seamstresses up all night between now and Wednesday to do it."

CHAPTER TWELVE

Cassandra looked into the cheval glass and could hardly believe what she saw. Her new gown moulded itself round her form and fell in soft folds to the floor. Made of satin, it had an overskirt of white gauze, with short puffed sleeves and a modest train. Moll had piled her hair on top of her head in an elaborate chignon which glistened in the candle-light, then wrapped a string of pearls round the base, to match the pearls at her throat. They had belonged to her mother and were the only form of jewellery she possessed, but tonight she wanted nothing more.

"You look like a fairy," said Moll gruffly.

Cassandra smiled and kissed her. But as she pulled on her gloves and went downstairs, she reminded herself that she was not going to an evening's entertainment. She was going to try and catch a killer.

Anne's carriage arrived promptly and Cassandra left the house. The night was fine, with just a suggestion of a breeze. A few stars sprinkled the darkening sky as she entered the carriage.

"I am so pleased you could join us," said Anne.

She was dressed in a beautiful gown of azure silk which was trimmed with matching ribbon.

"Delighted to see you again, my dear," said Charles affably.

"It was very good of you to invite me," said Cassandra.

"Nonsense. Any friend of Justin's is welcome in our house. We are so pleased the two of you met. You have been good for Justin, Cassandra," said Anne.

Cassandra did not know what to reply, and hastily turned the conversation.

"I am longing to see the Pavilion. The Prince has been busy altering it again, I believe," she said.

"He's turning it into a nabob's palace," said Charles, unimpressed.

"Charles!" remonstrated Anne.

"Well, you can't say he isn't," said Charles unrepentantly. "The stables look like they're from India, and inside the pavilion everything's Chinese!" He looked at Cassandra and winked. "I think he's losing his head over the place, myself, but don't tell him I said so, m'dear. Princes can be touchy, and if I offend him I might lose m'own head!"

Cassandra laughed.

"I haven't been to Brighton for a while, but it seems to me the Pavilion's growing grander every year," she said.

A simple house to begin with, the Prince had already extended it, changing the original farmhouse into a superior residence by doubling it in size. He had created a new wing mirroring the original building, and had joined the two with an impressive rotunda. Cassandra had watched its development with interest. The Prince had been altering it for most of her life, and there were rumours that he had plans for yet more changes.

It was not only the outside of the Pavilion that had undergone a number of changes. He had also redecorated it, reviving the fashion for chinoiserie.

"Indeed it is," said Anne. "He's added a conservatory and a new entrance hall—the first one was not grand enough for his tastes. And of course he's added to the gardens considerably. He bought the Promenade Grove a few years ago and turned it into part of his estate. It meant rebuilding the main London road further away from the Pavilion, but what is that to a prince? The road used to annoy him by passing right in front of the Pavilion—so little privacy!—and of course it separated the Pavilion from the Grove."

"Rebuilding the road!" said Charles, with a hearty guffaw.

"For a prince, rebuilding a road is but a trifle," said Anne reprovingly.

The carriage rolled through the streets and at last approached the Pavilion. Cassandra drank it in as they drew close. The starlight was eclipsed by the candlelight blazing out of the French windows. The windows themselves were magnificent. They were tall on the ground floor, with graceful proportions that added to the elegance of the façade. Those above were not quite so large, but their proportions echoed those of the windows below to create a harmonious whole. The building was covered in cream glazed tiles, giving it a bright appearance.

"I would like some Hampshire tiles myself," said Anne. "Just look how light they make the Pavilion look."

"But would you have such stables?" asked Cassandra.

"Well, they are certainly unusual," said Anne, "though I think they are not quite to my taste. But I would not tell the Prince so, for there is a rumour he is so delighted with them that he means to remodel the rest of the Pavilion in the Indian style."

The carriage rolled to a halt. Cassandra's mood sobered. Now was the time when her would-be assassin would be likely to strike. With all the jostling going on, a determined push would not attract notice, and if she was not careful she could find herself crushed beneath a carriage's wheels. But she was on her guard and the two footmen who flanked her as she climbed out of the carriage were on their guard, too. They kept their distance, allowing any attacker to come forward, but they kept a hawklike watch on her just the same. She began to walk ahead, looking to right and left. She saw no one she recognized, just a mill of people all dressed in their finest clothes, looking forward to an evening with their Prince. She crossed the drive. No one molested her. She reached the Pavilion. No one pushed her. She went inside . . . and then felt oddly deflated. If someone had attacked her it would have been over by now. Her attacker would have been in the safe custody of her guards. But now he was free to strike at any time.

She did not mean to let it spoil her enjoyment, however. This was her one chance to visit the Pavilion, and she meant to make the most of it.

As she went in, she heard a tinkling sound, and looking up she saw that there were bells hanging from the ceiling. They stirred with the breeze, casting silvery notes into the air. She and Anne exchanged glances. The Pavilion took opulence to new levels, and they were both intrigued as to what they would find next.

They went through the hall and found themselves in a long room that seemed to run the length of the Pavilion.

"Goodness," said Anne, looking round her. "This must be the Chinese Gallery. Justin's told me about it, but I never imagined anything so—unusual."

The gallery was immensely long and stretched away from them to both left and right. Chinese lanterns hung from the ceilings and were suspended from tall, carved supports. A mural of birds and bamboo fronds in a beautiful shade of blue covered the peach-coloured walls. Cassandra's eyes widened at the sight of a stove formed like a pagoda, and widened still further when she saw the life-size mandarin figures which were set into niches along the walls. They were dressed in real robes and they stood on bamboo cabinets, making them taller than she was and giving the gallery an exotic air. Looking up, she saw that even the ceiling was magnificent, being set with glass skylights painted in intricate designs.

"Have you seen the cabinets?" asked Anne in an undertone, as they walked past the elegant bamboo cabinets, which were fronted with panels of gathered red silk.

Cassandra was too overwhelmed to answer. Matching the cabinets were long sofas pushed back against the walls, and at the far end she saw a staircase made of bamboo.

"Well!" said Charles. And then again, "Well!"

Cassandra took it all in so that she could relate its splendours to Maria on the following day, but there was so much to see that she despaired of ever remembering it all.

At that moment, there was a stirring amongst the guests and, looking towards the end of the gallery, Cassandra saw the Prince himself appear. He was now over forty years old, and not as slim as Cassandra remembered him, but he was well made, with a pleasing face and an air of graciousness. His clothes fitted him exactly and were made of the finest cloth, making even the best-dressed of his guests seem to be wanting in this area.

He came forward most affably to greet his guests. Cassandra did not expect to be noticed by him, but he stopped in front of her and said, "So you are the beautiful Miss Paxton."

Cassandra did not know what to reply, but her evident confusion did her no harm with the Prince, who raised her from her deep curtsy, and said, "Charming, my dear."

He asked her what she thought of his home, and she replied truthfully that it was the most magnificent dwelling she had ever seen. He smiled, well pleased, and with a few more words, passed on.

Barely had Cassandra recovered from being spoken to by the Prince, however, than her heart began to beat even faster, for there, following the Prince, was Justin. He gave her a warm glance, but being in attendance on the Prince could do nothing more than bow before the Prince moved away.

Cassandra went through into the Grand Saloon, where a large party was gathered. The Prince liked to be amused, and had collected some of the ton's wittiest and brightest people around him. Gold and silver dazzled as the ladies' gowns caught the candlelight. The conversation was light and bubbling, and drifted up to the ceiling. Cassandra could imagine her brother in such surroundings. He had had an invitation once, on account of his wit, and he had sparkled. He had told Cassandra all about it, not just once but many times. He had been born to mix with princes, he had said.

There were a number of people she recognized. Lord Armington was there. He made her a bow when he saw her but did not approach. Miss Kerrith was there with her mother. The Prince had an eye for beauty, and she was not the only lovely young lady there. Matthew Standish, Justin's friend, was also there. He walked over to her casually, but Cassandra was not deceived. She knew he was alert, and that his seemingly casual glances round the room were in reality pointed, for he was one of the men who were making sure she was safe.

"Miss Paxton, how pleasant to see you."

"And you," she returned.

"What do you think of the Pavilion?"

"I think it's splendid."

"It is. But you haven't seen the best of it. The new banqueting room is magnificent. I expect you saw it as you arrived. It is in one of the most recent additions to the building."

"Oh, yes, I noticed it," said Anne.

A small group gathered round them. Matthew had many friends, and Anne, too, was well known. They talked amongst themselves until it was time for dinner. Then Matthew offered Cassandra his arm and led her in to the banqueting room. It was every bit as magnificent as the other rooms she had so far seen, and the sumptuous decorations were matched by an enormously long table draped in a snow white cloth and sparkling with glass and silver. Tall candelabras were set in a row down the centre, and chandeliers were suspended from the ceiling above.

"The meals are always extravagant," said Matthew to her in an aside, as she took her place at the table. "I hope you have a hearty appetite."

In fact she had none. She forced herself to look at the table and her close companions, but her eyes kept wanting to stray to Justin, who was sitting next to Miss Kerrith.

". . . French chef," Matthew said.

Cassandra collected her straying thoughts.

"Wonderful," she said, hoping her answer suited whatever he had said.

He smiled.

"I hear Lord Armington paid you a morning visit," he said nonchalantly, as tureens of soup were set on the table.

Cassandra looked surprised, but then realized that, as

she was being watched, all her movements and all the movements of those who visited her must be known.

"He did," she acknowledged.

"Armington's a fine man," he said.

"Indeed," she agreed.

"He's very popular with the ladies. It will be a lucky young woman who wins him for a husband."

Cassandra felt the conversation was becoming pointed, and did not reply.

"Don't you agree?" he asked.

"Yes, indeed," she said politely.

"Almost as lucky as the woman who wins Deverill," he said.

Cassandra had no more taste for her champagne. Putting her glass down, she said nonchalantly, "I believe Miss Kerrith is a likely choice."

"Do you? She's certainly very pretty," he said musingly, looking across the table to Miss Kerrith. "And she's an heiress. Some would say she would make him an ideal wife. However, I don't believe she's the wife for Justin."

"No?"

Cassandra relapsed into silence, knowing she had sounded both too eager and too hopeful.

"No. I think he deserves more than a pretty wife, even if she is an heiress. I believe he deserves the woman he loves."

And who would that be? Cassandra was about to ask, when she stopped herself just in time.

Matthew seemed to read her thoughts. He raised his glass and smiled, then, saluting her with his champagne, he took a long drink.

Cassandra could not resist a look at Justin. He looked up and their eyes met. Then the Prince claimed his attention and he was forced to look away.

The dinner was like nothing Cassandra had ever eaten before. The service was *à la française,* with all the dishes being arranged in the middle of the table so that guests could offer the various dishes to their nearest neighbours before helping themselves. There were four soups followed by four fish dishes, of which Cassandra had turbot served in lobster sauce whilst Matthew partook of the trout in garlic and tomatoes. She tried to catch the names of the various dishes when the fish was removed and the entrées were brought in, but her French had never been very good, and phrases such as *poulets à la reine, filets de lapereaux, petites croustades* and *filets de perdreaux à la Pompadour,* which seemed to trip off the tongues of those more used to the Pavilion, left her bemused. But when the dishes were arranged with all due ceremony in the centre of the table, she recognized woodcock, quails, partridges, pigeons, mutton and beef, all served in rich sauces which proved to be laced with Madeira, wine, port and truffles.

"Does the Prince eat like this every evening?" asked Cassandra, as once again the dishes were removed and pineapple jelly took its place alongside cherry tarts, chocolate soufflés and a host of other mouthwatering desserts.

"Yes, certainly when he has guests," said Matthew.

Cassandra glanced at her affable host, who was presiding over the meal, and thought it was no wonder his slim figure had not lasted. Nor was it any wonder his complexion was looking rather mottled. He had taken a great deal of wine, and was beginning to show signs of having drunk too much. His bonhomie, which had been evident throughout the meal, was becoming more exuberant, and Cassandra found herself hoping he would not speak to her after they retired from the table.

Leaving the banqueting room behind, they entered the drawing-room and Cassandra saw that cards, conversation and music were to be the order of the evening. A small orchestra was playing in the background, and guests began to pursue a variety of entertainments. Matthew excused himself, and Cassandra saw him walk across to Justin, who was no longer with the Prince, but was standing by himself at one side of the room.

"Well, I have never had such a sumptuous dinner in all my life," said Anne, joining her on one of the splendid sofas.

"Nor I," said Cassandra.

"I have eaten so much I can't move."

Charles laughed.

"Then it is a good thing there is no dancing. The Prince keeps a good table, and an excellent cellar. I've never drunk such marvellous wine in all my life."

"I'm glad you took it in moderation," said Anne, glancing at her host.

"He is used to it," said Charles, following her gaze. Then, changing the subject, he said, "Now, can I interest you ladies in a game of cards?"

~ ~ ~

Justin could not keep his eyes away from Cassandra. Was it only a few days ago that he had last seen her? It seemed like a lifetime ago. And yet here she was, now, in front of him, looking more beautiful than ever. Her blue eyes sparkled in the candlelight, and the pearls round her neck drew attention to the soft creamy skin of her throat. He was filled with protective feelings for her and longed to go to her, but he was at his Prince's pleasure. He had hoped the murderer would have struck by now, but the villain was probably waiting for the end of the evening, when the guests would be befuddled with wine and even less likely to notice a sly push in the dark.

He saw Matthew coming towards him. Making the most of the Prince's distraction, for the Prince was flirting with a pretty widow, Justin asked, "Are Cassandra's spirits good?"

"Yes," said Matthew. "She is bearing it very well. It can't be easy for her, knowing she could be attacked at any time and not knowing when."

"No, it can't," said Justin.

"She has plenty of courage," Matthew remarked.

"Yes, she has," said Justin, looking at her with admiration.

"And she knows her own mind."

Justin looked at him enquiringly.

"Most young ladies would jump at a chance to marry Armington, but not Cassandra."

"He proposed?"

"There could be no other reason for him to go down on one knee. Are you surprised?"

"No," said Justin truthfully.

"And . . ."

"And?" asked Justin, his heart stopping.

"And . . . I gave her every opportunity to say that she was engaged to him, but she said nothing. She turned him down."

Justin let out a long sigh, and his heart began to beat again.

"But I will say no more," said Matthew. He looked round the room. "We've another few hours yet before the party breaks up, but then we will need to be vigilant. It's when Cassandra leaves that the villain is going to strike."

~ ~ ~

Cassandra passed a pleasant hour playing cards, but as the evening drew on she began to grow uneasy. Despite the grandeur of her surroundings, some of the gentlemen had taken far too much to drink and an uncomfortable atmosphere was developing. The Prince of Wales was obviously drunk, but because of his rank no one could contain him as they could contain an ordinary gentleman, and when his bonhomie turned into something verging on exhibitionism Cassandra began to wish herself elsewhere.

"I think perhaps we should be leaving," said Anne to Charles.

"My dear, we can't. It would look most particular," said Charles, but he, too, sounded troubled.

There had been some rowdy practical jokes during the course of the evening, and Cassandra feared things were about to get worse. Her fears proved well founded when the Prince hit upon the notion of shooting with an air gun at a target set up at one end of the room. He called upon the assembled guests to watch him.

Cassandra stood up and began to move towards the door, but it was impossible to leave. Servants were coming in and out, bringing a target and other necessary paraphernalia in accordance with the Prince's orders, and she could not slip out.

"We will have to watch him," said a deep voice behind her, "but as soon as there is a chance to leave I will escort you to your carriage."

She knew before looking round whose voice it was. It was Justin's. She looked up at him as he moved to stand next to her.

"Is it often like this?" she asked.

"Unfortunately, yes," he replied. "When the Prince is bored, he must have entertainment, and we must all be ready to admire him, no matter how outrageous his ideas."

"I don't believe he'd notice if we slipped out now," said Cassandra, glancing at the Prince, who appeared to be occupied with telling the servants where to set the target. "But would that defeat the purpose of my being here this evening? Would my attacker try to kill me if I left early, when there wasn't a crush of carriages?"

"Probably not."

"Then I must stay."

"It would be impossible for you to do anything else," said Justin. "The Prince would notice if you tried to leave, and it would be unforgivable in his eyes. You would not be received in Brighton again."

The buzz of conversation died down, and Cassandra looked towards the end of the room, where the Prince was taking up an air gun. There was an expectant hush as he took aim. He fired. Despite his drunken state he managed to hit the target with commendable accuracy. There was a ripple of applause and many congratulations, and the Prince looked pleased. Cassandra felt her uneasiness growing, however, for having taken a shot himself, the Prince began to urge those closest to him to follow his example. Cassandra could only be thankful that she was no longer at the front of the room.

An elderly dowager was the Prince's first choice. She tried to protest, but he would not take no for an answer and put the gun into her hands. She was forced to shoot or risk his displeasure, but she did not know what she was about, and her shot hit the door. The Prince laughed and took the gun from her, handing it to the next person, a young lady with dusky curls—Miss Kerrith. Cassandra had no reason to like the young beauty, but she felt a surge of sympathy at Miss Kerrith's frightened face, for she, too, was forced to shoot. Miss Kerrith fared no better than the dowager. Her shot missed the target altogether, and she fired into the ceiling.

"If the Prince should look in this direction, drop your fan and then bend down to pick it up," said Justin in a low voice. "If his eyes don't alight on you, he will not choose you."

Cassandra nodded, grateful for his advice.

The Prince gave the air gun to another elderly lady and

applauded her shot, which by some miracle found its way to the target. Then he turned towards Cassandra.

Acting on Justin's advice, she dropped her fan, then bent down to retrieve it. She heard a shot ring out, and then stiffened as she felt a rush of air above her. This time, the shot had gone even further astray, and passed over her head. She turned instinctively to follow its trajectory, and saw a bullet lodged in the wall. Justin moved discreetly towards it and examined it. As he did so, his face grew pale. She knew why. Having lived with a dissolute brother she had witnessed similar drunken shooting matches, and she knew that the bullet had nothing to do with the air gun; it had come from a pistol.

She turned to Justin, but he was not looking at her. Instead, his eyes were scanning the room. Her gaze followed them, but saw nothing.

"Trouble?" asked Matthew in a low voice, coming up.

Justin showed him the bullet.

"Did anyone see anything?" asked Justin.

"No. Everyone's eyes were on the Prince and his victim."

"If I don't miss my guess, it's the murderer who suggested this game to the Prince. Do we know whose idea it was?"

"No, and it's no use asking," said Matthew. "The Prince will claim it as his own. This is getting too dangerous. We were prepared for an accident, but not a bullet, and we weren't prepared for such recklessness. To shoot a pistol, here in a crowded room . . ."

"He had the sound of the air pistol for cover," Justin remarked.

"It's still a reckless thing to do. It looks as though he's getting desperate."

Cassandra shivered.

"I want you to stay here with Matthew," Justin said. "I'm going to have your carriage brought round, and then I'm going to escort you home, whatever the Prince might think."

Cassandra wanted to finish what they had started, but at the same time she felt the danger was growing too high. She did not just have herself to think of. She had Lizzie, too.

Leaving Matthew by her side, Justin said, "Look after her," then chose a moment when the Prince was distracted and left the room.

"Ah! Standish!" The Prince's slurred voice rang out. "Just the man I'm looking for. Come and show us what you can do."

"It's all right. Go. I will be on my guard," said Cassandra.

Matthew reluctantly left her side. Cassandra edged into the middle of a large group of people. Anyone who tried to shoot her now would find it impossible to do so. Having done so, she felt a little safer.

"You had a narrow escape," came a voice next to her.

She turned to see Geoffrey Goddard.

"You know?" she asked in surprise.

He nodded. "I saw the Prince looking your way. It was a good thing you bent down, or he'd have chosen you next."

"Oh. Yes. Of course," she said, realizing he had been talking about her escape from being forced to shoot, and not her escape from death.

"The Prince often gets like this. It's best to keep out of the way and wait for him to tire of the game. He always does in the end. He will soon move on to something else. Would you care for a pinch of snuff?" he asked, taking a small and exquisitely engraved box out of his pocket.

"No, thank you," said Cassandra.

He flicked it open and took a pinch. As he did so, Cassandra noticed the inside of his wrist, and on it she saw he had a mole. It was the same mole she had seen on the wrist of the person who had tried to drown her. She felt herself grow cold. The murderer was here in the room, standing right next to her. It was Geoffrey Goddard. She glanced at Matthew. The Prince was handing him the air pistol. It would be some minutes before he would return to her side.

"Is anything the matter?" said Mr. Goddard.

"Oh, no, I was just hoping the Prince would not look

this way again," she said, wanting to back away from him but knowing that she must not let him know that she had recognized him.

"He's been a prince too long," said Mr. Goddard. "He has nothing to do, and he needs excitement. This is how he gets it."

"Yes, indeed," said Cassandra, growing more and more uneasy, and wondering how she was to get away from Mr. Goddard.

And then she was saved by one of Mr. Goddard's friends greeting him. Whilst he was distracted she slipped away from him, hugging the walls as she crossed the room. She went through a door into the hall and felt a surge of relief as she closed it behind her. She had escaped. Now she had only to find Justin and she could tell him what she had discovered before she left the Pavilion.

CHAPTER THIRTEEN

Cassandra looked about her, trying to get her bearings. She found that she was in the Chinese Gallery and did not know which way to go. She looked around for a footman, meaning to ask if he had seen Justin, but there was no one in sight. The gallery was empty. It was probably only the effects of her overstretched nerves, but she found the atmosphere oppressive. The Chinese mandarins set into niches no longer seemed exotic, they seemed ominous. Their faces were bland and their eyes were staring. Their robes were grotesque, making it seem as though at any moment they might come to life.

She felt her heart begin to beat more quickly as she began to traverse the empty gallery, her footsteps falling softly on the thick carpet. What if she lost her way in the strange corridors? What if she couldn't find Justin? Even worse, what if Mr. Goddard followed her into the gallery? She glanced over her shoulder nervously, but it was empty. She continued in what she hoped was the right direction, finding the silence unnerving.

The gallery seemed endless. It stretched ahead of her for miles . . . Miles? It could not be that long. And yet, although it was absolutely straight, she could not see the end of it. She felt the small hairs at the nape of her neck begin to rise. There was something very strange about the gallery. The bamboo murals and the Chinese lanterns seemed alien, out of place, and she longed to see something English. But all she could see was the endless corridor, stretching into an unimaginable distance . . . and then she came to a pair of doors. She stopped just before she bumped into them and laughed at herself. The doors were backed with mirrors! The endless gallery was a trick, and nothing more.

Feeling heartened, she opened the doors and saw the bamboo staircase beyond. She went forward cautiously. The staircase curved upward gracefully in two arcs, which met above as they led upstairs. She looked at the staircase more closely. It was not made of bamboo after all, but iron made to look like bamboo. The Pavilion, which seemed so beautiful and ethereal, was a fake.

She was about to turn round and retrace her steps when

she thought she caught sight of a slight movement behind her, out of the corner of her eye. She whirled round and looked back along the gallery but could not see anything. Could Mr. Goddard be hiding there? she wondered. Behind one of the mandarin statues, perhaps? It was not likely; surely there was not enough space for a man to squeeze behind them? But he could be hiding in one of the water closets, for the Pavilion was not only beautiful, it was equipped with the most modern conveniences, and water closets opened off the gallery's length.

She stood rooted to the spot, wondering what to do. If she went back along the gallery, then Mr. Goddard could suddenly appear and finish what he had begun. . . .

Should she go up the stairs? She went up the first few steps, but then hesitated. They led to the royal bedchamber, and she dared not intrude.

For a moment, she was paralysed with indecision, then giving herself a mental shake she told herself she had no choice. She would have to go back the way she had come. She went down the stairs and went slowly back. She peered into the water closets as she passed, and to her relief, they were empty. She had just checked the third one when Justin appeared, coming from the other direction.

"Cassandra! What are you doing here?" he exclaimed in horror. "Are you mad? Where is Matthew? You shouldn't be alone."

"Matthew's been monopolized by the Prince. I had to come. It wasn't safe in the drawing-room. When someone tried to drown me, I noticed a mole on their wrist. I've just seen it again. It was on Mr. Goddard."

"Yes, it makes sense. Goddard's too weak to be the ringleader, but he's always short of money. He gambles too much and nearly always loses. He's heavily in debt, and he's unscrupulous enough to do anything to get out of it. He must have had the idea of attacking you in the water after learning that Peter Raistrick was in the habit of dressing as a woman and going bathing."

"But we don't have any proof," said Cassandra.

"Don't worry about that. We have only to confront him and he'll talk. Now if we can only get him to tell us that it was Elwin who paid him, then we have them both. I want you to go home," he said. "The carriage will be at the door by now. We'll find Anne and Charles, and the three of you can leave at once."

"You'll let me know what happens?" asked Cassandra hesitantly.

"Yes."

"I have to return to my estate tomorrow. Lizzie is coming home and she is bringing a friend with her. I must be there to look after her."

"I know where it is. I'll come and see you there. I'll tell you everything as soon as I can."

"I understand," she said.

The door opened and Matthew came out of the drawing-room.

"I'm sorry, the Prince commanded me to shoot and I had no choice," he said to Cassandra.

"I know. I saw. It doesn't matter. We've found who the villain is."

Once they had told him, he nodded.

"I'll occupy Goddard whilst you see Cassandra to the carriage," he said to Justin. "Then we'll take Goddard."

"Agreed."

They went back into the drawing-room. The Prince was becoming bored with his shooting game and there were signs that it was coming to an end. Anne was already heading towards the door, with Charles beside her.

"Justin, thank goodness. And Cassandra. I think it's time we were going, before the Prince thinks of some other amusement."

"I've already called for the carriage," said Justin. "You'll find it waiting for you."

"What a relief!"

"I'll take you out," said Justin.

He offered Cassandra his arm.

Some of the other guests were beginning to leave. The Prince seemed happy for them to depart and was once more being the gracious host, bidding them farewell. Cassandra took her leave of him, and then went out to the waiting carriage. She settled herself down as Anne sat beside her, and Charles sat opposite her, then Justin closed the door. He bowed, bid them good night, and stepped back as the carriage pulled away.

"Well, that was a most unusual evening," said Anne, as she settled herself back against the squabs. "I am glad to have seen the Pavilion, but I hope I may not have another invitation for a long while. How the Prince can find such spectacles entertaining I do not know."

Cassandra agreed. Her evening at the Pavilion had not been at all what she had expected, but she had the satisfaction of knowing it had been successful. Mr. Goddard would soon be apprehended by Justin and Matthew. Tomorrow she would go back to her estate, and then . . . Then, despite everything that had passed between them, she found herself looking forward to seeing Justin again.

CHAPTER FOURTEEN

"Tell me all about it," said Maria the next morning, as she stripped off her gloves and untied the strings of her bonnet. "I mean to have the full story from you before you leave. You have no idea how envious I am! What was it like? Was it splendid, or was it vulgar? Was the Prince charming? What did you eat? What did you do?"

"It was splendid *and* vulgar," said Cassandra, helping Maria off with her spencer. "I've never seen anything like it. There were dragons everywhere, and lanterns, and bamboo. . . ."

Maria was agog as Cassandra told her all about the Pavilion's lavish decorations, and she was positively astounded as Cassandra told her about the target practice.

"Well! I'd heard some strange things went on at the Pavilion, but this is too much. I used to long to go, but now I think I am content with the assembly rooms."

"They are much more enjoyable, and much safer," Cassandra agreed.

"And how was your dress received? Did you have any compliments?" asked Maria, as she settled herself on the chaise-longue.

"One or two," Cassandra admitted, sitting next to her. "I was able to give Madame Joubier's name to Lady Ackerling and Mrs. Pendowan, so she will be pleased."

"She will indeed. Lady Ackerling is one of the best dressed ladies in Brighton and spends a fortune on her clothes."

They spent the morning talking about the Prince and the Pavilion, with all its splendid guests. Maria demanded a full account of all the ladies' clothes and Cassandra was happy to supply it, for it took her mind from other, less enjoyable, concerns.

At last Maria rose to take her leave.

"I wish you didn't have to go back to the country," she said. "Can't I persuade you to stay?"

"No. The house is ready for sale and I've put it in the hands of my lawyers. Besides, Lizzie will be home this evening. I must be there in time to welcome her."

"Then I must detain you no longer. But this won't be

your last trip to Brighton, Cassie. You must come and stay with us as often as you wish. We have plenty of room. Come at the end of the summer, before Lizzie goes back to the seminary, and of course you must bring her, too."

"I'd like to, but I've been away from the estate for too long as it is. You must come and stay with us instead."

It was arranged. In a few weeks' time, Maria would swap the seaside for the country and enjoy the late summer on Cassandra's estate.

Cassandra sighed as the door closed behind Maria. It was really happening. Her stay in Brighton was at its end. It should not bother her. Some terrible things had happened to her in Brighton, but there had also been some wonderful things. . . . Her thoughts turned to Justin. Her feelings for him had been in a state of almost constant turmoil since she had met him. Attraction and gratitude had developed into a desire to know more about him, from which had grown friendship, respect and trust. And then all those feelings had been swept aside by the desolate hollowness she had felt when she had learnt he had been in part responsible for her brother's death. It had taken her into a valley of darkness, but she had come through it, climbing out of it as her need for Justin's help had once more turned to friendship, trust and respect. And through those feelings something stronger had been threaded, something that made the thought of leaving him almost impossible to bear.

She would soon be seeing him again, she told herself. He would come to her estate and tell her who had paid Geoffrey Goddard to attack her. He would let her know that the villain had been apprehended, so that she would not have to fear being attacked again. But then . . . She had thought, at one time, he had feelings for her, but had they really been there, or had she imagined them, reading more into them than he felt? Matthew's comments had led her to suspect that her feelings for Justin were returned, but did Matthew really know how Justin felt?

Shaking aside her gloomy thoughts she set about finishing her packing. John loaded the coach, Moll packed the hamper, she locked the door, and they were on their way.

~ ~ ~

Justin rode out of town towards a seedy lodging house some miles north of Brighton. Things had not gone according to plan the night before. Having returned to the drawing-room in the Pavilion, he had been unable to apprehend Geoffrey Goddard: the Prince had taken a fancy to the young man's snuff box and the two had been deep in conversation. He had been forced to watch as they began drinking together, falling deeper and deeper into a drunken stupor as the night progressed. Knowing he would get no sense from Goddard in such a state, Justin had been content to follow him from the Pavilion in the small hours of the morning and then set a watch on him. But now Goddard would have slept off the worst of his excess and the time had come to apprehend him.

Meeting Matthew at the end of the road on which the boarding-house was situated, he entrusted his horse to the care of an urchin, and when Matthew had done the same he approached the house. A sharp rap on the door brought an unkempt woman to the doorstep. Clutching her dirty shawl around her shoulders, she pushed a greasy strand of hair out of her eyes.

"What d'you want?" she asked suspiciously.

"We are here to see Mr. Goddard," said Justin.

"And oo might you be?"

"A friend."

She looked him up and down, then her glance passed to Matthew.

"What's it worth?" she asked.

Justin handed her a sovereign, and she opened the door.

"You'd best come inside."

Justin and Matthew went into the dingy hall.

"Up there," said the woman, nodding towards the staircase. "Third door on the right."

"Thank you."

They went up the creaking stairs and stopped outside Goddard's door. It was painted a grey colour that had once been white, and here and there the paint was coming off.

Justin knocked on the door. There was no reply. He knocked again.

"Go away," came a thick voice from the other side of the door.

"Goddard, it's Deverill. I want to talk to you."

"Come back later."

"No. Now."

"What are you doing up at this unearthly hour?" asked Goddard, coming to the door. He was dirty and unshaven, and he was still dressed in his clothes of the night before.

"We want to talk to you."

He looked from one to the other of them, then shrugged and let them in.

"Drink?" he asked, picking up a bottle and waving it at them.

"No. You've had enough," Justin said, taking it out of Goddard's hand.

"Going too far, Deverill," said Goddard, reaching out for the bottle.

"You can have it back when you tell me what I want to know," said Justin.

Goddard looked as though he wanted to protest, but then he collapsed into a chair and said, "And what might that be?"

"I want to know who paid you to kill Miss Paxton?"

"Wha . . . ?" Goddard looked from one to the other of them, and then a hurt look came into his eye. "Me? Kill little

Cassie? I don't know what you're talking about. I wouldn't do anything to hurt little Cassie."

"I'm not in the mood for games," said Justin pleasantly, but with a smile that could have frozen the sea. "I want to know who paid you."

Goddard looked at him muleishly.

"If you tell me what I want to know, I'll let you go," said Justin. "You're the lowest of the low. In fact, you're slime. But you wouldn't have tried to kill Cassandra unless you'd been paid. So who paid you?"

Goddard looked at Matthew.

"This is a joke?" he said.

"No joke," said Matthew.

"So who was it? Elwin? Was he afraid of her? Afraid she knew something that could harm him?" demanded Justin.

"Elwin's never been afraid of anything in his life," Geoffrey sneered. "He didn't want to see her dead. He wanted her to take a lover and he intended to get a payment for making the introduction himself, but if that didn't work, he was going to abduct her and sell her outright. It would be easy to do. She's got no family to look out for her."

Justin's hands balled into a fist.

"Oh, hasn't she?" he said dangerously.

Matthew put a restraining hand on his arm.

"Who paid you?" he said to Goddard. "If it wasn't Elwin, then who?"

Goddard began to laugh.

"How much is it worth to you?" he asked.

"Nothing," said Justin evenly, regaining control of himself. "But it's worth a great deal to you. If you tell us, we'll let you go. If not, we'll hand you over to the authorities for attempted murder."

"You haven't any proof," Goddard jeered. "You don't know it was me."

"Cassandra saw the mole on your wrist when you tried to drown her," said Justin.

Goddard's face fell. Then he recovered.

"Lots of people have moles," he said.

"In that case, you have nothing to fear. No doubt you'll be released without charge."

Goddard looked into the two faces in front of him and wavered.

"Yes, well, I might be, and I might not. There might be some who'd believe it."

"There might indeed," said Justin. "In that case, you could find yourself locked up for a very long time. I hope he's made it worth it. Tell me, what's he paying you?"

"Not enough to go to prison," said Goddard, reaching for the bottle in Justin's hand.

Justin gave it to him, and took it back when he'd had a drink.

"Then I suggest you tell me everything," said Justin.

Goddard reached for the bottle again, but Justin withheld it.

"All right," said Goddard, slumping back in his chair with a scowl. "Just give me the bottle and I'll tell you everything I know."

~   ~   ~

Cassandra's journey was a pleasant one. The day was fine and the weather was warm. Once back at her estate, she set about helping Moll and John unpack the coach but once it was done she found it difficult to settle to anything. There was plenty to do, she reproved herself. The garden was overgrown—she really must ask Mrs. Windover to teach her the difference between plants and weeds, so that she could tidy the flower-beds in front of the house—and there had been a leak in the attic. Lizzie's room needed airing, there had been a fall of soot from the drawing-room chimney and one of the dining-room curtains had rotted through and fallen down. She would have to see to it all before Lizzie and Jane arrived that evening. But for the moment, she wanted to escape from her problems.

Turning her back on them, she went out of the house. She had time for a walk before she had to face up to all the household difficulties. She went across the lawns and took a snaking path through the shrubbery at the back of the house. It was cool between the vast shrubs, but once out from their shadow the sun hit her with full force. The clouds parted to reveal a hot yellow sun and a clear blue sky.

She turned her footsteps towards the chestnut grove. It was a favourite walk of hers and it would be cool beneath the trees. Once she had walked its length, she would go back to the house and face her chores.

She cut through another swathe of shrubbery and turned towards the grove . . . only to feel her throat constrict. Someone had been cutting the trees down! The villain who had broken into her house! Had he attacked her grounds as well? She shook away the idea as being too unlikely. But someone had been felling the trees. The closer she went, the more wanton the destruction seemed. The trees did not appear to have been used for wood. They simply lay where they had fallen. There were no drag marks to show that any of them might have been taken away, no evidence of fires, nothing. But why would anyone do such a thing?

She drew closer. As she did so she saw Mr. Brown, her neighbour, standing there. She wondered if he had had similar problems on his own estate, and if he had come to warn her there were vandals in the neighbourhood. At that moment he turned round. He looked startled to see her.

"Mr. Brown," she said.

"Miss Paxton. I thought you were in Brighton."

"I've come home," she said. "Do you know what happened here?"

"Oh, yes, I know," he said.

"You do?"

"Yes."

There was something odd about the way he said it, and something strange in his smile. It was quite different from normal. There was usually something ingratiating in it, but now it was almost jeering. She knew she ought to ask him to tell her what had happened, but somehow she did not want to know. She was about to make an excuse to leave him when he said, "I cut them down."

"You?" she asked in surprise.

She had the alarming feeling he had gone mad. She wondered whether she should remonstrate with him and tell him he had had no right to do it, but there was a glint in his eye that frightened her and she glanced round instinctively, working out her best way of escape.

"Are you going somewhere?" he asked mildly.

"I was looking for Moll. I said I would meet her here," she said.

"No you didn't," he said. "You're trying to work out how to escape. You're frightened. And so you should be. Your life is worthless. I've been trying to have you killed for weeks, and it's only a matter of time before I succeed."

"You?" she said, astonished. "But why?"

"Why? For the treasure, of course. But you don't know about the treasure. Let me tell you about it. A long time ago,

275

after the Civil War, one of your ancestors fled to France, but he buried the family treasure before he went."

"I know. But—"

"Ah, you know. That's a surprise. But you don't know where it is. You can't do, otherwise you would have dug it up yourself. There are some advantages to living with one's nose stuck in a book—yes, I heard your sister saying that. It wasn't very polite of her, was it?"

Cassandra was grateful that Lizzie was not there, and would not be home for hours. At least her sister was safe.

"You see, that's how I found out where the treasure was buried, by using your library. The treasure's under one of the chestnuts, and I'm going to find it."

"So that's why you've been cutting them down," said Cassandra.

"Of course. And why I've been visiting you so often. I needed access to the library so that I could continue to read Joseph Paxton's journals and gather my information. I didn't want to borrow them, or you might have wondered why I took an interest in them." He gave an unpleasant smile. "I'm sorry to disappoint you, but it was never your charms that attracted me. I heard a whisper of the treasure one night when your brother was in his cups. It was at the local tavern. He spoke of it, and said that Joseph Paxton had buried it, but not where. He mentioned something about a journal. It was too much of a risk for me to try anything at the time, because your brother was rather wild and unpredictable, but once he died I knew my hour had come. I visited the house as often as I could and read every one of Joseph's journals whilst you thought I was choosing a book to borrow. Alas, the journals never said which tree the treasure was buried under, so I decided I would have to cut them all down. I borrowed a book on trees so that I could find out what a chestnut looked like, and then I was ready to begin."

"So that is why you asked me to marry you," said Cassandra. "So that you would have access to my land."

"Yes. I fear I made a bad job of it or you would have said yes, but I have never known what to say to ladies."

"I wouldn't have married you whatever you had said," remarked Cassandra in disgust.

"You would have preferred a pretty face, I suppose," he said. "Women are so foolish. It's a pity you didn't say yes. It would have been better for you if you had. I would have married you and then I would have cut the grove down as a surprise for you—'I am planning a treat for Cassandra's birthday,' I would have said to the neighbours—"

"You had worked it all out," said Cassandra, horrified.

"Of course. 'A new vista,' I would have said—those books on gardening I borrowed were always talking about vistas—and then, surprise, when I cut down the trees, I would have discovered the treasure. *My* treasure, because as my wife, everything you had would have belonged to me. I would have been rich! You needn't think I would have kept everything for myself. I would have been generous. I would have given you a new gown and a necklace. Women set great store by such things. But you refused me, and so I had to think of another way of getting what I wanted. And then you announced you were going to Brighton. Your visit gave me the chance I needed. No one would notice what was going on when you were away. Once I found the treasure, I could take it to London and sell it, and no one would ever know anything about it."

"But I would have noticed the felled trees as soon as I returned home," said Cassandra.

"Which is why you had to die. The servants never come down here, and nor does Elizabeth, but you often walk here. If I could have been sure you would not return until I had cut down all the trees, I would have let you live. I could have pretended I knew nothing about the damage. But I did not know how long you intended to be away, and if you had returned before I had cut them all down and I had not found the treasure, I would have lost my chance for ever. And so you had to die. The beauty of it was that you were to have an accident in Brighton, so your death would not be connected with the trees if anyone had noticed they had been felled. But that fool Goddard seems to have made a mess of things. A pity. I thought he had made a mess of it once before, when you returned unexpectedly. I broke into your house at night, intending to kill you whilst you slept, but you had locked your door. I visited you on the following day, intending to kill you, but John was with you. Then you revealed that you were returning to Brighton and I decided to stand by my original plan. I did not want your murder connected to the estate. But now it can't be helped."

"The coach," said Cassandra, remembering that the wheel had come off her coach on her first journey to Brighton. "Was that you?"

"Yes. It was another of my own efforts. If the wheel had come off whilst the coach was going down a hill it would have overturned and you would have been pitched out, very possibly breaking your neck."

"I should have realized before now. I knew the accidents I'd been having were more than accidents, but it never occurred to me that the very first accident I'd had could have been an attempt at murder, too."

If she had only realized it, she might have realized that the man behind the murders was not Mr. Elwin at all, but someone closer to home, she thought.

"So now you know everything," said Mr. Brown, taking a step towards her.

"There's no need to kill me," said Cassandra, backing away.

He looked amused.

"No? If I leave you alive, you won't tell anyone, I suppose? Oh, come now, Miss Paxton, you know I can't let you live. You have no proof I'm behind the attempts on your life, but you'd prosecute me for cutting down your trees and claim the treasure as your own."

"There is no treasure," she said. "Joseph's son dug up all the chestnut trees when he returned from France. He knew that was where his father had buried it. But he found nothing. His father had given it to his mistress. Either that, or it had been taken by looters during the Commonwealth."

"It's no good," he said with an unsettling smile, "you can't save your life like that."

"But it's true," said Cassandra. "Look at the trees. They were planted at the end of the seventeenth century. They're barely more than a hundred years old. The ones that were here before that were planted in the thirteenth century. They would be huge by now."

"Dear me, what nonsense. Cut down all the trees, indeed. I've read John Paxton's journals. He makes no mention of cutting anything down."

"My father kept some of the journals in the study," said Cassandra. "They contained useful information on running the estate. You did not see them. Look at the trees," said Cassandra again.

"A good try, but you know no more about trees than I

do," he said. "The only time you tried to do anything with the garden you managed to kill most of your shrubs. You do not know how old they are."

"Why do you think we never cut down the trees if the treasure was here?" she asked.

"Because you didn't know where to look."

"Of course we did. We knew the story. Rupert knew the story. He also knew that the chestnuts had been dug up and no treasure had been found. It was just a pity he didn't tell you all of it."

"This will get you nowhere," said Mr. Brown. He took a pistol out of his pocket and levelled it at her. "I've wasted enough—"

"Put it down."

The voice took Cassandra completely by surprise. So engrossed had she been with Mr. Brown and her efforts to reason with him that she had not noticed a new person enter the scene, and her heart leapt as she saw that it was Justin. She was very glad to see him—and then wished he had not come, as Mr. Brown pointed the pistol at him.

And then, in front of her horrified gaze, before she had time to think, let alone react, she saw Mr. Brown's finger squeezing the trigger and he fired.

Time froze. She heard the crack of the pistol and turned her head to look at Justin, saw a look of surprise cross his face and then he staggered backwards as his hand rose to his chest. He stumbled and then began to crumple, his legs buckling as he fell to the ground.

"No!"

Cassandra cried out in anger and frustration and despair. She ran towards him but she seemed to be moving so slowly. It took for ever for her to reach him, and when she did, it was too late. His eyes were closed and he was pallid.

"No," she said, hot tears running down her cheeks.

She sank down beside him, forgetting her own danger, forgetting everything but Justin.

"Justin, Justin my love," she said, as she took his hand and looked into his pale face. "Speak to me, my love. Oh, Justin, don't be dead."

Her eyes dropped to the bullet hole in his coat. It was right over his heart. She unfastened his coat with shaking fingers—and then his hand closed gently around her wrist, and he said, "Don't you think you should wait for our honeymoon before you do that?"

She stopped what she was doing, barely able to breathe, then slowly she looked into his face.

"Justin? Justin!" she said, as his eyes opened. "Justin!" she said in relief.

He gave a slow smile.

"But how . . . the bullet . . ." She sat back on her heels, her mind reeling.

He sat up.

"I think I owe my life to this."

He reached in his waistcoat pocket and pulled out a gold locket. It was badly dented. It had acted as a shield and had prevented the bullet from reaching his chest.

"Mama's locket," she said, astonished, taking it from his fingers. "But how . . . ? where . . . ?"

"I won it from your brother at the gaming tables," he said gently. "I meant to give it back to you, but once I'd opened the locket and seen your portrait, I couldn't bear to part with it."

"You saw . . . So that is how you recognized me," she said, remembering the first time they had met.

"Yes." His eyes softened. "I recognized you. And then I fell in love with you."

"Love?" she said breathlessly.

"Yes, Cassandra, love," he said softly. "I've been in love with you for a very long time."

"I thought . . . I hoped . . . but you said nothing."

"I felt I had no right to speak, not whilst the truth about Rupert's death lay between us. Even when I knew you had forgiven me for his death I did not know if you would ever be able to love me. I didn't know until I heard you call me 'my love'."

He put up his hand and stroked her face.

"I have nothing to offer you, except my title and myself. My fortune is gone. We will not be rich. But if you give me a chance, I will make you happy. Well, Cassandra?" he asked, his voice gentling as he took her chin between his thumb and fingers. "Will you give me that chance?"

"Oh, yes," she said.

She felt herself melting as his lips covered hers and all the promise of their earlier meetings was fulfilled. It was exhilarating and engrossing and wonderful.

At last he pulled away. His eyes were glittering with unsated desire, but he said, "No more. Not until we are married, at least. Name the day."

"We have nothing to wait for," she said. "We will marry as soon as it can be arranged."

He kissed her again, and only let her go when a cough broke the silence.

Cassandra looked round, to see that Matthew was just finishing tying Mr. Brown's hands. She blushed.

"I did not see you there," she said, feeling suddenly awkward.

"No, I rather thought you hadn't noticed me," he said with a grin.

Justin laughed and stood up. He helped Cassandra to her feet, then put his arm around her waist.

"It seemed a good idea to bring Matthew along," said Justin, turning to her. "He comes in useful from time to time!"

Matthew laughed at the sally.

"If not for me, you two would have been murdered whilst you kissed each other."

"I can think of worse ways to die!" said Justin.

Cassandra smiled.

"Who is the local justice?" asked Matthew.

"Sir William Fielding," said Cassandra. "He lives in the big red brick house at the start of the village."

Matthew nodded. "I passed it on my way. I'll take this villain there, and I'll leave you two to arrange your wedding."

"At which you will be the groomsman," said Justin.

"Not even Napoleon could stop me," said Matthew.

"Take my horse," said Justin.

Matthew nodded. Propelling Mr. Brown forward, he made for the end of the grove. Looking down the length of trees, Cassandra saw two horses. She watched as Mr. Brown mounted clumsily, his hands tied behind his back, and then saw Matthew mount his own horse. The two of them rode away, with Matthew leading Justin's horse by the reins.

When they had ridden out of view, Cassandra and Justin began to walk back to the house, arm in arm.

"I am glad Matthew is to be our groomsman," said Cassandra. "I will have Maria as my matron of honour. She will be delighted. And Anne must be a matron of honour, too, if you think she would like it."

"She will like it above anything. She told me weeks ago that she wanted me to make you my wife."

"She did?"

"Yes. As soon as she'd met you, she knew I should marry you."

"It's a pity you didn't speak out then," said Cassandra.

"Is it? Would you have said yes?"

She hesitated.

"Perhaps not. I knew that I had strong feelings for you, but they were confused. It wasn't until I saw you being shot that I knew I loved you."

"Then we have something to thank Mr. Brown for, after all."

They walked across the lawns and went into the library through the French doors. As they did so, Cassandra heard Lizzie's voice.

"It's Lizzie. She must have arrived early. She wasn't meant to be here until this evening."

A moment later her sister was running across the room to greet her, whilst Jane hung back shyly. On seeing Justin, however, Lizzie stopped. She looked at Cassandra enquiringly.

"I have taken your advice, Lizzie," said Cassandra with a smile. "I have found a husband!"

"I knew you would," said Lizzie. She turned to Justin, beaming. "Are you a marquess?" she asked.

"No, sadly not," he said. "I am merely an earl."

"Never mind," she said consolingly. "I'm sure it's very nice to be an earl." She turned to Cassandra. "Don't worry, Cassie, when I marry my marquess, I won't expect you to curtsy to me, and neither of us will curtsy to Jane."

"Jane is going to marry a duke," Cassandra explained to Justin, as Jane hung awkwardly by the door.

"Ah. A very good idea," he said to her kindly.

Lizzie was not impressed.

"I don't think so. Dukes are always old and fat. Are you rich?" she said to Justin.

"Lizzie!" said Cassandra.

"No, alas not," he said.

Lizzie gave a heavy sigh.

"Then it will be up to me to restore the family fortune by marrying a *rich* marquess."

"That is very good of you," said Cassandra, "but before you save us all from ruin you will oblige me by showing your guest to her room and then washing your hands before supper."

"Oh, if I must." Lizzie ran over to the door and took Jane's hand, then stopped and looked back. "I'm glad you're not going to marry horrid Mr. Brown."

Cassandra and Justin exchanged glances, but remained silent. It was better for Lizzie not to know what had happened.

"So am I," said Cassandra lightly.

Lizzie and Jane ran out of the room.

"You won't mind Lizzie living with us?" Cassandra asked, as she and Justin walked over to a deeply buttoned sofa and sat down.

"Of course not," he said. "She's part of the family. It's where she belongs."

Cassandra looked round the much-loved room.

"I would like to live here when we are married," said Cassandra. "I know the house is shabby, but I don't think I could bear to leave it. Will you mind?"

Justin stroked her palm.

"Not at all. I think it's a good idea. We can rent out my house in Brighton. It won't be enough to pay off the mortgage on the estate, but it will bring us some luxuries. For my own sake, I don't mind being poor," he said, looking into her eyes, "but I'm sorry I have so little to offer you."

"Not so little. So much," she said.

He smiled down at her. Then, taking her in his arms, he kissed her.

"I thought we were going to wait until we were married," she said, when at last she emerged from the embrace.

"So did I. It seems we were both wrong," he said.

Then he kissed her again.

EPILOGUE

Cassandra could hardly believe it was almost five years since she and Justin had been married. So much had happened in that time. First there had been the wedding, which had been a lavish affair. Justin's sister had insisted on providing them with a wedding breakfast on her estate and had hired a French chef specially for the occasion. She had arranged a sumptuous meal which had been crowned by a cake made out of spun sugar, of which Lizzie had eaten so much that she had made herself feel sick. Afterwards, when the September daylight had faded, they had watched a spectacular firework display. Then had come the honeymoon in London, with all the joys of shops and theatres, and all the pleasures of getting to know Justin not just as a man but as a husband, and their return to their estate, where they had begun their married life. Justin had continued to pursue the traitors' ringleader, finally finding evidence against Mr. Elwin and bringing him to justice. And now here she was, with three children and a happy, if impoverished life.

Cassandra turned her attention back to Maria's letter, which she was reading in the library, curled up on the window seat.

My dear Cassandra,

We haven't seen you for an age. We do so hope you will come and visit us. Come soon! I am so sorry you have to sell Justin's house, but I know that renting it is no longer good enough for you so I will give you what help I can, Cassie dear. It seems no time at all since you were selling your own house. It's hard to think you and Justin have been married for five years. I am so pleased you married him, Cassie, I always said he was just the husband for you.

Cassandra smiled.

"Something interesting?" asked Justin, who was sitting at the desk and wrestling with the accounts.

"Maria is reminding me that she always said you were the husband for me."

He laughed. "After Lord Armington, I believe."

"Lord Armington was very charming," Cassandra teased him.

"Be careful. I'm still not past the days of being jealous! What else does she have to say?" he asked.

"She says that she will give us what help she can to sell the town house," she said, as her eyes scanned the page.

Justin threw down his quill.

"Are you sure you're happy with this idea?" he asked. "Once it's sold, we won't be able to buy it back again."

She uncurled herself and put the letter aside.

"Yes, I am. As long as you are not having second thoughts?"

"No. We can put the money to better use. Lizzie is almost sixteen now. She will be needing a season, with clothes and fans and everything else that goes with it. And our own children will be needing things soon. They are growing up."

"Jay is four," said Cassandra, with a quirk at the corner of her mouth, "and Victoria is three. And the baby is not yet one."

"There you are, they will be needing horses before you know it," he said, laughing. Then, becoming serious he said, "No regrets?"

"None," said Cassandra.

She went over to the desk and put her arms round him, kissing him on the forehead.

He pulled her on to his lap and kissed her thoroughly on the lips.

"Mmm," she said.

"And talking of our children, where are they?" he asked, as he reluctantly let her go.

"In the garden with Lizzie. They are making the most of the fine spell of weather."

She looked out of the window at the sky. It had patches of blue, but already the clouds were gathering again. There had been a storm in the night, and it seemed as though they were in for more bad weather.

"You had better fetch them in," said Justin, looking at the sky. "I think it's going to rain heavily soon. It's very different from the summer we met. I seem to remember it being sunny every day then."

Cassandra straightened her gown and went out into the garden. She had filled out since she had met Justin, assuming a more matronly figure, but her eyes were as blue and her hair as golden as ever. She had given these attributes to Jason, their son, a little boy everyone called Jay, but Victoria had inherited her father's dark hair and green eyes.

She saw little Jason now with Lizzie, sitting on one of the paths that ran through the shrubbery, but there was no sign of her daughter.

"Where's Victoria?" she asked.

Lizzie looked up, and turned clear blue eyes on her sister.

She's very beautiful, thought Cassandra with pride. Even more beautiful than I was at her age.

Lizzie's figure was curvaceous, and had already caused

interest amongst the local boys, but Cassandra meant Lizzie to have a wider choice of husband than was available in their own small neighbourhood. When the time came, Lizzie would have a London season—and perhaps find a handsome marquess!

"She was here a minute ago," said Lizzie.

Cassandra looked round for her daughter, then saw her by the roots of the oak that had blown down in the night.

"It was lucky the tree was no nearer the house," she said. "If it had landed on the roof, we would have had to spend a fortune in repairs."

She went in search of her daughter, and soon saw her running towards her.

"What have you there?" said Cassandra, looking at the sparkly thing round Victoria's neck. As she drew closer and scooped her daughter into her arms, her eyes grew wide.

"Victoria, where did you get this?" she asked.

Victoria waved an arm back in the direction of the oak tree.

"What is it?" asked Lizzie, standing up and dusting her hands, before joining her sister.

"I'm not sure," said Cassandra.

Lizzie took Victoria.

"These look like rubies," she said in surprise.

"I know."

They looked at each other.

"You don't think . . ." began Lizzie.

"I'm not thinking anything," said Cassandra.

She went over to the toppled oak, closely followed by Lizzie. There, in a hole beneath the roots, was a treasure trove. Rubies, sapphires and diamonds winked in a ray of sunshine. Pewter plates were mingled with bracelets and necklaces, whilst goblets had strings of pearls spilling out of them.

Lizzie climbed into the hole and came out with an armful of gold and jewels.

"It's the treasure," she said.

"But it was buried beneath a chestnut tree," said Cassandra uncomprehendingly. "Joseph's journal said so."

"But Joseph wasn't a gardener," said Lizzie, beginning to laugh. "He was like all the other Paxtons. He couldn't tell one plant from another—or one tree either, it seems!"

"And all this time the treasure's been lying here, just waiting to be found," said Cassandra. "I must tell Justin. He's about to write to his lawyer and tell him to go ahead with the house sale."

"We won't need to sell anything now," said Lizzie, draping jewels around her neck. "I can have a wonderful season, with silks and satins and lace. Oh, Cassie, just think what it will mean. And I can wear the family jewels," she said, picking up a diamond brooch.

"You are far too young for diamonds," said Cassandra. "The brooch is mine!"

"Then I will have the pearls," said Lizzie.

"An excellent choice. You can have them remodelled in the latest style."

"And we can sell some of them," said Lizzie. "There are so many we won't notice. I can have new clothes, and so can you, Cassie."

"And so can the children!" said Cassandra. "And not just clothes, but horses, too. Justin can fill the stables and the children can have ponies to ride."

She scooped Victoria up in her arms.

"Come," she said, "let's show Papa what you've found."

She carried the little girl back into the house.

"I find I've changed my mind about selling the Brighton house after all," she said.

"Hm?" He did not look round.

She walked over to the desk and put Victoria in his lap.

"Hello, sweeting," he said, kissing her on top of her head.

He still did not look up from his figures.

"I think we should keep it," she said.

Victoria took the rubies from her own neck and hung them round her Papa's.

"Pretty," she said.

"Very nice," he said absently, fingering the rubies. Then his fingers stilled. He took his eyes from his ledger and looked at the necklace, then looked up at Cassandra.

"Where . . . how . . . ?" he asked.

"We've found the treasure."

"No!"

"Yes. Under an oak tree!"

He sat back in his chair and laughed.

"An oak tree! So Joseph was no more a gardener than you are!"

"No."

"But is there more?" he asked, fingering the rubies.

"Much, much more," she said. "We're rich. Just think what this will mean."

"It means we will be busy," he said.

"Yes, we will." She picked up Maria's letter. "I had better write to Maria. Instead of going to Brighton to visit her, I think she had better come here to visit us instead!"

Amanda Grange lives in Cheshire, England, and has written many novels including *Darcy's Diary* and *Captain Wentworth's Diary*. Visit her website at www.amandagrange.com.